"Dad was a man driven to succeed, at any cost."

Yes, even at the cost of another man's life, Chloe thought privately.

"That must have been hard on all of you."

"It had its moments," he said sparingly. "Dad died a couple of years back. Now I've decided that his opinion doesn't matter. I'm here for me. To live my best life. It's why I go for what I want when I see it and I make no apology for that."

"And why should you. Isn't that how we should all live? Striving for what we want? Honestly, as long as we don't do harm to others, isn't that the way to live our best lives?"

Miles cocked his head and looked at her carefully. "I'm more and more convinced that fate put you on that collision course with me yesterday. Does that sound corny?"

Oh, it was fate all right.

* * *

Black Sheep Heir by Yvonne Lindsay is part of the Texas Cattleman's Club: Rags to Riches series.

Dear Reader,

To me, family is everything. You can have your differences, but when push comes to shove, it's family that can hold us together when everything else is falling apart. This year has been particularly hard for our family with the death of a much-loved aunty and ongoing health battles with other family members. But at the end of the tunnel was the light of our much-anticipated granddaughter to lighten our hearts and remind us that family continues to be everything.

In *Black Sheep Heir*, Miles Wingate, who is estranged from most of his family for wanting to go his own way in life, is called to action when things start going from bad to worse in one of the Wingate companies. Miles drops everything to assist his family. Chloe Fitzgerald has her own agenda. Her family was destroyed by Miles's dad years ago. Growing up with her mother's bitterness toward the Wingates being a constant refrain, Chloe wants to see her mother find happiness more than anything. Will revenge against the Wingate family be enough?

I hope you will enjoy reading this installment in the Texas Cattleman's Club: Rags to Riches continuity. And special thanks to my fellow authors for being so amazing to work with.

Happy reading!

Yvonne Lindsay

YVONNE LINDSAY

BLACK SHEEP HEIR

HARLEQUIN
DESIRE

Special thanks and acknowledgment are given to
Yvonne Lindsay for her contribution to the Texas
Cattleman's Club: Rags to Riches miniseries.

Recycling programs
for this product may
not exist in your area.

ISBN-13: 978-1-335-20919-1

Black Sheep Heir

Copyright © 2020 by Harlequin Books S.A.

This edition published by arrangement with Harlequin Books S.A.

For questions and comments about the quality of this book,
please contact us at CustomerService@Harlequin.com.

Harlequin Enterprises ULC
22 Adelaide St. West, 40th Floor
Toronto, Ontario M5H 4E3, Canada
www.Harlequin.com

Printed in U.S.A.

Award-winning *USA TODAY* bestselling author **Yvonne Lindsay** has always preferred the stories in her head to the real world. Married to her blind-date sweetheart and with two adult children, she spends her days crafting the stories of her heart. In her spare time she can be found with her nose firmly in someone else's book.

Books by Yvonne Lindsay

Harlequin Desire

Wed at Any Price

Honor-Bound Groom
Stand-In Bride's Seduction
For the Sake of the Secret Child

Marriage at First Sight

Tangled Vows
Inconveniently Wed
Vengeful Vows

Texas Cattleman's Club: Rags to Riches

Black Sheep Heir

Visit her Author Profile page at Harlequin.com, or yvonnelindsay.com, for more titles.

You can find Yvonne Lindsay on Facebook, along with other Harlequin Desire authors, at Facebook.com/harlequindesireauthors!

I dedicate this book to the memory of our darling aunty Joy, who will be forever missed but carried in our hearts forever.

One

"Vultures!"

Miles Wingate balled up the newspaper in his hand and tossed it across the dining room in a controlled burst of fury. The crumpled ball bounced on the polished wooden floor and skittered to rest against the molded baseboard. Even then, he could still see the glaring headline that had destroyed his appetite for anything remotely resembling breakfast.

WINJET FAILS SAFETY INSPECTION!

The syndicated article had cut far too close to the bone, exposing serious flaws in safety procedures at the WinJet aircraft manufacturing plant in Texas. At the very least, the fines would be massive. At the worst, the entire plant could be shut down. The fact that his late father's cost cutting measures and often-underhanded tactics had come home to roost didn't cause Miles much surprise. But when it meant his elder twin brothers, who headed Wingate Enterprises, and the rest of his family had to bear the brunt of it? That infuriated him in ways that he hadn't experienced since long before he'd turned his back on the family business and moved to Chicago.

Still, his dad had been dead and buried for two years. Surely his brothers, Sebastian and Sutton, should have picked up on the discrepancies, which had led to the fiery disaster at the plant last month. Three workers had been seriously hurt. The lawsuit that had followed could easily be handled, but the subsequent internal investigation findings that had now led to a joint OSHA and FAA investigation becoming fodder for the media? That meant serious trouble for the company.

"Not my circus, not my monkeys," Miles ground out.

And, because he couldn't tolerate mess, he strode across the floor and picked up the balled-up paper and tossed it in the recycling bin. Even without the reminder there in front of him, he knew he had to do something to get this irritating itch out of his system. He shouldn't let it bother him that his family name was being dragged through the mud. After all, he'd made his choice to step away from everything associated with Wingate Enterprises a long time ago.

He'd used his knowledge and his contacts to establish his own company, Steel Security, and he had a team of employees that he valued and respected.

People who took security, both personal and cyber, as seriously as he did himself. He would never let anything happen to any of them, if he could help it, and if something did occur, you could bet your last dollar that he'd hold himself accountable until proven otherwise. As far as Miles was concerned, his responsibilities began and ended right here, in Chicago, with his team.

But that didn't stop him from feeling as if he shouldn't do something for his family. Wingate Enterprises had enjoyed many years of escalating success on the backbone of the employees who worked for the company. His family had a duty to look after those people. That they hadn't, and that it had come down to something as basic as safety, stuck in Miles's craw like a dry husk. The injured workers were well within their rights to sue. Everyone deserved to come home safely at the end of their shift. But something about the whole matter didn't sit right with him. He knew his brothers were nothing like their dad. They didn't cut corners, and they respected people. He should call them, at least.

"Not my problem," he reminded himself.

He had to get out, clear his head. It was the start of the new month and a Wednesday morning, his work-from-home day. His usual routine meant he'd go for an hour-long run, come home, shower and lose himself in his work with no interruptions. If he didn't go for that run, he knew he'd never be able to settle. The phone calls could wait. Already dressed for exercise, he grabbed his earbuds, strapped his phone to his upper arm and headed out the door.

Pounding the pavement between his town house and Lincoln Park, he finally felt his body begin to relax into a calming rhythm. And with every yard he covered, he could feel the distance between the disturbing news back in Texas and the life he'd chosen here in Chicago widening. Yeah, this was exactly what he needed.

Today was set to hit the low nineties but the temperature right now was still comfortable. Despite how things had started, this was going to be a good day.

Chloe Fitzgerald checked her watch again. He was late. Every Wednesday at exactly 8:00 a.m. Miles Wingate ran in the park. Every Wednesday but this one, by the looks of things, she thought ruefully. It just went to prove, even with the best-laid plans, there was always something that could throw a wrench in the works. She strode back and forth on the pavement, debating whether or not to give up on her idea for today and to regroup. Find another way to engineer that *chance* meeting with the man who would ultimately lead her to the vengeance her family so richly deserved.

She'd waited so long for this. Years, in fact. Tears of frustration suddenly pricked at her eyes. Why had he changed his routine today of all days? Was it because of the story that had been plastered all over the news? Reading the report that the illustrious Wingate family were under investigation for unsafe practices had given her so much satisfaction. After all, it was past time they got their just desserts. It wasn't fair that her family had suffered while theirs had prospered—especially when the late Trent Wingate had built a generous proportion of WinJet's success on the back of her father's own business after driving her poor dad to take his own life.

Growing up with the stigma of having a parent who'd committed suicide had left its scars. Scars that had deepened with her mother's bitterness at having to pack up the life she'd known in Texas and accept charity from distant family here in Chicago to get them where they were today. No, their life had not been easy. And there'd been plenty of time for Chloe to think about the Wingates and what she'd do if she ever got the chance.

Discovering that the younger Wingate son lived and worked in Chicago, versus being enfolded into the Wingate Enterprises umbrella, made him more accessible. And, as a Wingate, Miles was no less culpable in her book. Yes, she was all about visiting the sins of the father onto the sons and daughters of that callous bastard, Trent Wingate. His progeny had taken their privileged lives for granted for long enough. It was time they saw their sainted father for the scoundrel he truly was.

The family could ill afford more bad press, and Chloe had plenty to dish out. All in good time of course. To get the ball rolling, she'd contacted the reporter who'd broken the first story about the fire at the WinJet plant with an offer to give him more information about the family at grass roots level. She'd given him her background and told him about what Trent Wingate had done, but the reporter had said the story lacked immediacy. He could maybe use it in conjunction with something else—something more current. So she'd created her campaign.

First, she planned to get close to the family. Then, when she was well entrenched, she'd show them, through the media, exactly what their father had done to hers. And, ultimately, teach them how much it hurt to be betrayed. But first, she had to get close to the family, and if Miles Wingate didn't turn up for his regular Wednesday morning run, her plans would fall apart.

Which was *unacceptable*.

She'd spent hours and hours on this. Scheming and waiting to be able to implement her plan until she was on summer break from her job as an elementary schoolteacher. Now it seemed foolish to have pinned all her strategy on an initial chance meeting during his regular Wednesday morning run. But it had made so much sense to her at the time. Bump into him. Strike up a conversation. Let the conversation lead to a drink or dinner, maybe. She wasn't ugly and she knew Miles wasn't in a relationship right now. Surely he'd take her bait?

He was a creature of routine. She'd taken heart from that. Except today he'd varied that routine. Normally Miles would have passed this section of path by now and been heading up toward the monument. Chloe ceased her pacing and stood still, searching the area around her for the tall, familiar figure she'd been scoping out for the past couple of weeks.

Maybe she should just start running. Maybe he'd taken a different route today for some unknown reason. Maybe she'd bump into him somewhere else on the many paths that lined the park. So many maybes. She hated anything to be unsure. She'd had quite enough of that in her life. Miles Wingate's routine had reassured her—underscored that she was doing the right thing.

Routine was the backbone of her existence, too. It was one of the reasons why she'd become a teacher. The sweet young faces in her class might change with the start of each school year, but the basics remained the same. Structure was everything. Planning was everything.

She needed a new plan.

Chloe spun around and started to head back toward her car, at the exact same moment as a tall, blond-haired, male figure came toward her and barreled straight into her. The impact knocked her clean off her feet and drove the breath from her lungs. She landed smack on her bottom on the path and uttered a startled "Oh!"

"I'm so sorry," the man began. "Are you okay? Are you hurt? Can you stand?"

She looked up. The morning sun was like a halo behind him and she couldn't quite make out his features, but there was something in his deep, masculine voice that she recognized from the online video clips she'd seen about him and his company.

Miles Wingate, in the flesh.

Her jubilation at tracking down her quarry was tempered with the fact she could still barely draw in a breath.

"A minute," she managed to squeak out, and raised a hand with her forefinger up.

He knelt on one knee in front of her. At this angle she could now see his face, and she felt as if she'd been sucker punched all over again. The man, in person, was so much...*more*... than he was on-screen or in news bulletins.

"I'm okay," she said eventually, even though her heart continued to race in her chest. Due more to his proximity than to their collision. "Look, I'm sorry. I got in your way. I didn't hurt you, did I?"

He smiled. "I'm fine. I'm more concerned about you. Are you sure you're all right? That was quite a fall."

She shifted gingerly. Her butt was tender but there was no way she was admitting that.

"I was more winded than anything, I think," she said with a smile. "Again, I'm really sorry about all of this. I should have been looking where I was going."

"You did kinda change direction all of a sudden, but I should have been more careful, too." He straightened and extended a hand. "May I help you up?"

She hesitated a second, caught by the old-fashioned courtesy in his Texas drawl. She and her mom had lived in Illinois so long now, she'd almost forgotten what that sounded like.

"Thank you."

Chloe placed her hand in his and allowed him to help her to her feet. His hand was warm and strong, and despite her intentions, she felt a zing of awareness travel up her arm. He let her go the minute she was upright. A gentleman to the core. It would have been so easy to have allowed their contact to linger, but he hadn't. There was absolutely nothing inappropriate in his touch, although a curl of curiosity in the back of her mind made her wonder if he'd felt that same electric charge that she had.

"Is that blood on your hand?" he asked, jolting her out of her reverie.

Chloe turned her hand palm up. She *was* bleeding a little. Must have been from when she put her hand out behind her, to try and stop her fall. Actually, now that she came to think of it, her wrist was a bit sore, too.

"It'll be okay. It's nothing serious."

"May I look?"

Again, that courtesy. She proffered him her hand and caught her breath as he cradled it in his own.

"Is that sore? Me touching you like this?"

"A little," she admitted.

Actually her wrist was now beginning to hurt a lot, and to swell, too.

"I don't like the look of this," Miles Wingate said. He looked up at her with a small frown furrowing between his sharp green eyes. "You need to get this seen to. Let me take you to a medical center."

"No, seriously, I'll be fine. A bit of ice, a compression bandage—that's all I need."

"Look, I feel responsible for your injury. Let me help you."

Chloe chewed her lower lip. She knew exactly who he was, but he had no idea of that. What would a regular woman do in this situation? She certainly wouldn't instantly act as if she trusted him. Would she?

"No, it's okay," she forced herself to say, and reluctantly pulled free of his touch. She winced a little and cradled her wrist in her other hand. "My car is parked nearby. I'll be fine."

Miles straightened. "Look, I know you don't know me from Adam, and despite having bowled you clean off your feet, I really mean you no harm. Let me introduce myself properly—Miles Wingate, at your service. And you can trust me. I actually work in security, so I totally get why you don't want to accept my help. Thing is, I feel bound to offer it to you and to see that you accept it. But not in a creepy way, of course."

He smiled at her then and looked so earnest she couldn't help but smile back in return.

"Chloe Fitzgerald," she murmured. "And thank you for your honesty."

"Will you let me walk you to your car?"

"That would be lovely. I just need my—" Chloe looked around for her cell phone. She'd had it in her hand when she'd fallen. A few moments later she spied it lying on the path a couple of yards away. The screen was a maze of cracks. "Oh no," she cried.

Miles picked it up and ruefully studied the smashed screen.

"Look, this is entirely my fault. I'll replace it for you. It's the least I can do."

Chloe didn't quite know what to say. She felt like she ought to protest, but she certainly couldn't afford to buy a new phone right now.

"I—" she started, but Miles cut across her protest before she could fully form the words.

"Ms. Fitzgerald, allow me to replace your phone. Believe me, it's no bother."

There was something in the way he said the words that rankled. It was a combination of the expectation that she wouldn't dare to refuse, blended with the fact that the purchase of a new device for her would hardly be a blip in his budget. She swallowed the bitter retort that immediately sprang to mind and forced herself to smile.

"Please, call me Chloe. And, thank you. I wouldn't normally accept such a generous gift but I'm totally lost without my phone."

"As are we all," he said with another drop-dead gorgeous smile.

Like an idiot, she felt herself automatically smiling back again. Oh, he was too much. Too good-looking, too polite—just too *everything*! And every cell in her body that wasn't currently throbbing in pain was reacting to him in ways she hadn't anticipated.

"Where are you parked?" Miles asked, oblivious to the turmoil she was going through.

Chloe mentioned where she'd left her car, and together they walked along the paths.

"Do you run here often?" Miles asked after a few steps.

Chloe giggled.

"What? What's funny about that?"

"Oh, just a new take on an old line, don't you think?" she quipped, looking up at him.

Doing so, unfortunately meant she wasn't fully looking where she was going and her foot caught on an uneven section of pavement. Miles was quick to reach out and steady her and, she noted with reluctance, just as quick to let her go again. Even so, the warmth of his hand and the gentleness of his touch had left her wanting more.

Ridiculous, she told herself. She'd only just met him. She wasn't the kind of girl who reacted like this to anyone. Her mostly tame relationships to date had been few and far between. Juggling the responsibilities of teaching with supporting her mom, who was prone to depression, Chloe usually didn't feel as though there was much of her own self left to go around. Most men didn't understand her relationship with her mother and, until that one special guy did, she was happy to wait. Besides, being in a relationship would complicate her plans for vengeance.

A shiver of apprehension prickled along her spine. *Vengeance.* It was such a deliberate and often cruel word. Did she have what it took to go through with it?

Two

Miles walked beside the slender woman he'd sent flying. How could he have been so careless? He wasn't in the habit of bowling over blue-eyed petite blondes any day of the week. At least not literally. And she was definitely the kind of woman he would normally notice. Even now he was deeply aware of the lightly sunkissed tone of her skin, the gentle curves of her body beneath her running clothes and the way her lips parted slightly on a sharply indrawn breath. Not that he should be looking, he silently castigated himself, nor reacting he realized, as he felt his own physical awareness of her sharpen. He really felt he owed her a great deal more than a new phone—and he wasn't too pleased with how her wrist was looking now, either.

"This is me," she said.

She'd stopped by an old model sedan that looked as though it had seen better days. He peered inside, noting the stick shift.

"Are you going to be okay with that?" he asked, pointing to the gear lever.

"Oh. I didn't think of that."

"The pain is getting worse, isn't it?" he pressed.

She looked reluctant to admit it but eventually nodded.

"I'll drive you to get it checked out. Last thing you need is another accident today."

"I don't want to impose. I'm sure you have better things to do."

"Better than rescuing a damsel in distress?"

She laughed, just as he'd intended.

"Okay then. Thank you."

He didn't realize, until she agreed, just how much he didn't want to say goodbye to her.

"Keys?" he asked, holding out his hand.

"On top of the front wheel."

"You're kidding me, right?"

She gestured to the tight-fitting running pants she was wearing. "No pockets."

"Those things usually have a pocket at the back, don't they?"

"Budget version," she said with a light shrug of her shoulders.

"As a security consultant, I can't begin to tell you how risky this is," he grumbled, retrieving the keys from their not-so-hidden spot. "You're lucky your car is still here."

"I know, but I figure it's so old, it's hardly likely to attract trouble."

He opened the passenger door for her and it gave a loud creak of protest. "I can see why," he commented wryly.

She laughed again, and the sound made something begin to unravel at the center of his chest. He closed the door once she was inside the car and got in on the other side.

"I guess your mother told you never to get into a car with a stranger when you were little, right?"

"She did. Are you suggesting I'm not safe here with you?"

Her words made every protective instinct bloom from deep inside of him.

"I want to reassure you that you are completely safe with me."

"Good to know," she said before awkwardly fastening her seatbelt. "I'd hate to have to hurt you."

His lips tweaked into a smile. "Hurt me?"

"My mother also sent me to self-defense classes. You'd be amazed at what I can do with one good hand."

He nodded slowly and turned on the ignition. "Good to know."

After he drove to the nearest urgent care center and parked the car, Chloe turned to face him.

"Look, I really don't want to take up too much of your time. You don't need to stay with me. I'm sure once my wrist is bandaged up, I'll be okay to drive."

"No problem, and, as to your wrist, we'll let the doctor decide. Okay?"

Two hours later they were back at the car with Chloe protesting every step of the way.

"You didn't need to pay for me, Mr. Wingate. I have insurance."

"Miles."

"What?"

"Call me Miles," he said with a smile. "And, yes, I *did* have to pay. If it wasn't for me, you wouldn't have been hurt in the first place."

"It was my own silly fault," she reminded him half-heartedly.

She was looking pale. The examination of her wrist had been painful, but they'd both been relieved when the X-ray had shown nothing was broken. But clearly she was tired now.

"How about we call a truce on whose fault it was? I'll see you home and then I'll arrange your new phone to be delivered."

"No, I have to draw the line at the phone. I'm sure I have an old one somewhere I can charge up until I replace my other one."

"I won't hear of it. Look, Ms. Fitzgerald—"

"Chloe. If I'm to call you Miles, you must call me Chloe."

"Chloe." He liked the way it tripped off his tongue. In fact there was an awful lot he liked about this woman. "One thing you're going to learn about me is that I am a very determined person."

She quirked a brow. "Does that mean you don't listen to other people?"

"Oh, I always listen. It's how I work out what people really need. In my line of business it would be a mistake not to listen."

"You said you're in security?"

"Yes, both personal and online."

"Just you?" she asked.

"No, I have a team of experts working for me."

"So, you're the boss of everything?"

He felt a grin pull at his lips. "Well, maybe not *everything*. But I am the boss of Steel Security, so trust me, paying for your medical bills and for a new phone won't cripple me financially."

She looked him straight in the eyes. From here he could see her pale blue irises were flecked with gold. They were the kind of eyes he could stare into for quite some time and happily get lost.

"Based on your experience as a security expert, would you advise a woman on her own to allow a stranger, like yourself, to take her home?"

Miles laughed. "Not under normal circumstances, no. In fact, I would advise against it most strongly. However, if you would like to speak to my assistant at the office, I'm sure they could vouch for my identity and, I hope, my trustworthiness."

She continued to stare at him, then gave a little nod. "As a schoolteacher, I've learned to be a pretty good judge of character, and I think I'll be okay with you. I accept your kind offer."

"Excellent. Now, I'll take you home so you can rest up."

"And what about you?" she asked. "How will you get home?"

"I'll call for a ride. Honestly, it's no bother. So? Where to?"

She gave him her address and he raised his brows.

"Midlothian? You came a fair distance to run in the park."

She shrugged and looked out the window. "I like the park."

Miles continued to look at her, but she kept her gaze firmly outside. He couldn't help but admit it. She intrigued him in a way that he didn't want to ignore, but there was something about her that made his senses prickle, too. Something he couldn't quite put his finger on. Something that made him curious on a professional level as well as a personal one.

Miles turned on the car and backed out of the parking space before heading toward Midlothian. This time of day the trip would probably take around forty minutes. Again, he wondered why she'd chosen to come to Lincoln Park this morning, since it was so far away from where she lived.

She shifted her gaze from out her side window and back toward him. "I'm always looking for places to take my class on day trips. The Lincoln Park Zoo is one of my favorite places to go. That's why I was at the park this morning."

"Hey, no problem," he said, wondering why she sounded a little defensive.

"Did you want to come in for a coffee or something cool to drink before you call your ride?" she asked unexpectedly, changing the subject.

Miles was on the verge of refusing but then thought better of it. "Sure, that'd be great. Thanks. Although, as a security expert, I would advise against it."

She laughed. "I'm pretty sure you're safe."

They got out of the car, and he followed her down the path to the small single-level house. She let them into the house, which looked neat and tidy, and was furnished with the bare minimum. A couch and an armchair in the living room, together with a wall-mounted TV and a small coffee table. They went into the kitchen, where Chloe one-handedly filled the carafe on her coffee maker and then tried to measure out the coffee.

"Here, let me do that for you," Miles said, stepping forward.

Their hands brushed as she passed him the scoop, and his eyes flicked to hers. Her pupils had dilated, and that tiny fact made him more than a little curious. He was definitely attracted to her, and it gave him no small measure of satisfaction to see that attraction reciprocated. He knew right then and there that, one way or another, he would be seeing more of Chloe Fitzgerald.

Chloe leaned back against the kitchen counter and watched as Miles moved around the compact space while he made their coffee.

"You're pretty good at this knight in shining armor thing," she teased as the machine spluttered, signaling the coffee was done.

Miles grabbed the carafe to pour out their coffee. "I try to be good at everything."

"I've had a couple of kids over the years like that." She looked at him, noting the intent way he concentrated as he did everything. "Challenging kids. Does that make you a challenging adult?"

He barked a short laugh. "You'd have to ask my family about that. Or maybe my staff. I'm sure there'd be any number of them happy to fill you in."

"I'll bear that in mind."

She accepted the mug he passed her and walked through to the living room. He followed soon after and sat beside her on the couch. Chloe took a sip of her coffee.

"Good coffee, thank you. I'm sure I do exactly the same thing as you and yet mine never tastes as good."

"Ah, it's an old Wingate family secret," he said with a slow wink.

And just like that, the easy camaraderie they'd been building shattered. Chloe forced herself to keep a smile on her face, but it was difficult when she'd just been so soundly reminded of exactly who it was that was sitting here in her house with her. She'd allowed herself to be lulled by his care of her after her fall, but she had to keep her wits about her.

"So, I guess that means you're not sharing your secrets?"

"I'm an open book. I don't have any secrets. Seriously, though, it's all about how you measure the coffee."

She laughed. "And that's it? No magical ingredient hidden up your sleeve?"

He held out his arms in his short-sleeved T-shirt. His biceps and forearms were beautifully shaped, and muscles rippled beneath his tan as he turned his hands up then back again to show her he had nothing hidden anywhere.

"As you can see, nothing," he said.

Oh, there was no way there was "nothing" about Miles Wingate. He certainly was *something* and, despite her throbbing wrist and sore palms, she was completely and utterly aware of him as a man. A very attractive man at that.

"You mentioned being a teacher," he said. "Do you work near here?"

"Yes, at a school a few blocks away. It works well living here. I can walk to school during the semester when the weather's good. A bunch of kids often walk with me."

"I bet you're popular."

She pursed her lips. "Oh, how so?"

"Let's see. From my first impression of you, you're warm and friendly and don't want to cause a bother. You listen well and you're not demanding or pushy. How's that for starters?"

"You discerned all that from just this short time?" she queried.

"It's my job to read people and situations. I know there's also a lot about you that you're holding back.

You choose your words carefully, as if you don't want to accidentally give anything away."

Chloe felt her eyes widen. Did he read her that well? Maybe this whole idea of hers was about to head to hell in a handbasket.

"You're good," Chloe admitted non-committally, taking another sip of her coffee.

"I make it my business to be good." Miles drained his coffee mug and stood up. "I'd better call that ride."

"I feel terrible to have taken up so much of your day. I am sorry."

"Hey, no need. I wanted to make sure you'd be okay. And, now I know where to have your new phone sent to."

He gave her a smile and went through to the kitchen, where he washed out and dried his mug and returned it to the shelf where he'd taken it from originally. So far, he'd done nothing to be faulted on, Chloe realized. He'd been friendly, chivalrous, and he made a darn fine cup of coffee. And she wanted to bring his family's world down around their ears? Her conscience pricked at her.

She knew this wouldn't be easy, but she had to remain committed. Chloe thought about the family portrait of her parents and her that she kept on her nightstand. It was a constant reminder of what Trent Wingate had destroyed. Three lives irrevocably changed because of Wingate's greed. And that greed had continued to fester as his fortune had grown. Nothing had ever been enough.

Chloe needed to keep that truth in the forefront of her mind because no matter how charming Miles Wingate was turning out to be, he was, first and foremost, one of Trent Wingate's children. Much of the privilege he'd grown up with and taken for granted every day of his life was due to his father stomping all over hers.

All her life she'd witnessed her mother's deep unhappiness, and she would give anything to see her mom genuinely smile again. Maybe, just maybe, if Chloe succeeded in hurting the Wingates, even if it was just a little, it would be enough to break her mom free of the miserable state she'd lived in over the last nineteen years.

They'd both suffered long enough.

Three

Miles parked his Audi e-tron quattro at the curb outside Chloe's house and looked at the sad little building. She didn't belong there. The sagging guttering, the peeling paintwork on the clapboard exterior and the general air of neglect to the rental home told him more about her landlord than he wanted to know. The house could best be described as a renovator's dream.

His fingers tightened on the leather-wrapped steering wheel. Yes, he knew his feelings about Chloe's living conditions were irrational. They were also none of his business, if he was being totally honest with himself. But, and it was a *big* but, he wanted to make it his business.

From the moment he'd knocked her over this

morning, he'd wanted to make sure she was okay. And the more time he'd spent with her, the more he wanted to ensure that things went right for her. Sure, he'd been taken by her pretty face, her blond hair and the clear blue of her eyes. Her figure was pretty damn fine, too. Hell, he was a heterosexual male and she was absolutely his type. He'd have to have been blind not to notice her—although, in hindsight he hadn't noticed her soon enough not to cause her hurt.

But there was more to it than just that. He'd seen the vulnerability in her gaze when she'd looked at him. Sensed the reserve behind the words she'd so carefully chosen before she'd allowed him to help her. Caution was a good thing. His entire business plan revolved around it, after all. But there was something about Chloe that made him want to slay dragons for her. She drew on every protective instinct he'd never known he'd had. And that surprised him.

Every relationship he'd had, to date, had been based on equal footing. Women as strong mentally and, occasionally, even physically as he was. None of them had needed his care or protection in the same way he sensed that Chloe might. Not that she was a complete damsel in distress—in fact she was probably far from it.

She was a schoolteacher. He had no doubt she could control a room of potential delinquents with a smile or a frown—she had that air about her. But there was something else, something that lingered beneath the surface. A sadness. A sense of something broken. Something that called to him to fix it.

Miles had never experienced this kind of attraction before. An intriguing blend of physical awareness together with that special something else that made him want to know everything about her.

The aroma of the Thai takeout he'd picked up on the way here teased his nostrils. Enough thinking. Time to do. He got out of the car and grabbed the takeout bag and tucked the box with the new phone under his arm. Oh sure, the store had offered to courier it out to Chloe for him, but he'd wanted to make the delivery himself.

Miles could hear the sound of music from inside the house as he strolled up the path to the front door. And was that singing? Well, he supposed it might be singing but it sounded like it had more in common with a nine-tailed cat in a room filled with rocking chairs. He raised his free hand to the front door and knocked firmly. Instantly the noise stopped.

A few seconds later, the door opened and Chloe stood there, cheeks flushed and eyes wary.

"Oh," she said. "You're back."

"I'm glad to see that fall today didn't affect your vision," Miles said with a grin. He held up the take-away bag. "Dinner."

"I wasn't expecting you. I thought you were the courier."

"Tonight, I'm whatever you want me to be."

The flush on her cheeks deepened and a laugh gurgled from her throat. "Did that come out exactly as you meant it to?"

He laughed in response. "To be honest, not exactly. It sounded much better in my head."

Chloe stepped aside and gestured for him to come in. "I thought as much. You'd better bring that all in then."

He noticed she was still wearing her arm in a sling, but she'd changed from the plain white one she'd left the clinic with, to a large, multicolored silk square instead.

"I like the sling."

She half smiled. "White is so yesterday, don't you know?"

"How's your wrist?"

"Feeling a lot better, to be honest. I think the pain relief medication helps."

Miles went into the kitchen and spied some sandwich fixings on the counter. "Dinner?"

She rolled her eyes. "Well, it was going to be until you showed up."

He gave the stale bread and jar of peanut butter a disparaging look. "I'm glad I did, if that's what you call dinner."

"I wasn't really hungry." She sniffed the air appreciatively. "But what is that delicious smell?"

Miles opened the bag and removed the containers. "Green curry and vegetables with jasmine rice and a prawn pad Thai."

Chloe gave him a sharp look. "Are you sure you're not some kind of mind reader?"

"Not the last time I looked. What makes you ask?"

"Those are my favorites. I can never decide between them."

"Then you can have some of each," he told her. "But first, I thought we could set up your new phone. I've already charged it for you so it's ready to go as soon as you've transferred all your data."

"Miles, you really are too generous." She looked rueful. "I'm not sure I can accept all of this from you. After all, we hardly know one another."

Miles stilled. "Would you rather I leave? Have I come on too strong?"

"Too strong?"

"I'm going to be honest with you, Chloe. I know I never knew you existed before today, and it's going to sound strange, but I feel like we were meant to meet. I'd like to know you better and I'm not the kind of man who likes to waste time." He blew out a breath and looked her straight in the eye. "When I see something I want, I go for it. Life is too damn short to spend it wondering what if. But that said, I'll go if you prefer."

Chloe caught her breath at the earnest expression on his face. From anyone else, that could have come across as stalkerish, but for some reason his words sounded just right. *And*, the little voice in the back of her mind reminded her, *it means he's falling into line with what you have planned without any hard work on your part. You were meant to meet today, after all. He just didn't know why—yet.*

"I…" She blinked rapidly, unsure of what to say. "Please stay. I'm just not used to people like you."

"Like me?"

"So sure of what you want," she clarified. "Most folks I know are too afraid to reach for what they dream of."

"Everyone has their reasons."

"And yours are?"

He'd been in the process of putting their takeout in the oven to keep warm, and he closed her oven door and straightened.

"My reasons are simple. I never want to be beholden to anyone for anything. I got where I am on a vehicle of my own making and I have dreams I'm still reaching for. Anyone can ride along with me if they want to and if they're prepared to work hard. I'm not into forcing compliance. I'm not into unreasonable expectations. I lay all my cards on the table and if people don't like what they see, they're free to go."

Chloe weighed Miles's words carefully. His outlook was basically the antithesis of everything she'd ever known about his father. The senior Wingate had been known for his ruthlessness. It must have been so galling for the senior Wingate to have been stricken by the first debilitating stroke he'd endured five years ago.

For a man so in control of everything in his life to be reduced to relying on others for even his most basic human needs? It would have been torture. And yet when Chloe had heard the news she'd found it difficult to summon even an ounce of sympathy for him. Knowing the man had died in his sleep two years ago had only served to stoke the fire of her anger. Her father had had no such luxury.

And now she had his youngest son in her crappy kitchen, espousing his live and let live policy on life. She'd always thought the apple didn't fall far from the tree when it came to family dynamics and the way people grew up. But it seemed that Miles was different. For starters, he'd made his success here in Chicago, far from the Wingate empire that was centered in Royal, Texas, and which had arms that reached out internationally through aviation, oil and hotels.

Had she made a mistake in targeting the closest, easiest option for her revenge? No, she decided, she couldn't think that way. Whatever Miles was like, it was his family she was after. She wanted them all to feel and know pain, like she'd felt and known it. To suffer like her mother had—and still did, locked as she was in her grief for the past.

Chloe forced a smile to her face. "Well," she said as brightly as she could manage. "That sounds fine to me. I have a small confession to make. I've done a little research on you."

There, it was out in the open. Not a lie, although the implication she made was that the research was recent, whereas in actuality it was of far longer standing. Miles began to grin and Chloe felt a twinge of something entirely feminine deep inside her body. The man was far too attractive for his own good. And probably hers as well.

"Research, huh? And what did you find out?"

"Enough to know that I'm intrigued by you, and I'm wondering what the heck it is about me that's made you come back tonight."

He took a step toward her and she felt a flutter in her chest as he stood close enough for her to inhale the fresh, crisp fragrance he wore. It was clean and enticing, like a breeze off the lake on a summer's day. It made her want to lean in a little, to lift her face, to see whether he'd respond to the cues and do whatever came next. When Miles lifted a hand to push an errant strand of hair off her cheek she felt as if his fingertip had burned a brand of ownership across her cheek.

"Y'know, I've been asking myself that same question. But it all comes down to me knowing what I want when I see it. Like I said before—I know its early days, Chloe, but there's no question that I want you. And I want to get to know you better while you decide if you want me, too."

His gaze dropped to her lips and she saw the flare of hunger in his green eyes. Her body flooded with heat in response, but then he turned away—leaving her standing there with her lips slightly parted and her brain and body on overload. He'd been about to kiss her; she knew it, and yet he hadn't. Had he decided it was too soon, or had she been sending the wrong message? Or was he just some kind of tease?

No, she doubted it was the latter and she knew for a fact she'd just about had foot-high neon signs blinking over her head shouting at him to do it. To close the scant distance between them and to take her mouth with his. And he'd been about to. Every feminine instinct in her told her that was so. Then, for some reason, he hadn't. If anything, it intrigued her even more.

She continued to watch him as he turned his attention to the box containing her new phone and knew she wasn't mistaken that he was as deeply affected by that short interaction as she'd been when she realized there was the slightest tremor in his hands.

"It's the latest version of the phone you had already," he said, looking up at her. "You should be able to transfer the information from your old one easily."

"That's great. Thank you. Like most people, I have my life on that device."

"Do you back up?"

"Yes, religiously."

"Good. And everything is strongly password protected?"

She nodded. "And changed regularly."

"Good. You'd be amazed at the number of people who aren't. They really ought to know better, too."

She shrugged. "I learned my lesson when I was in college. I had my notes for one of my courses on my phone. I dropped it in a toilet."

Miles laughed. "Uh-oh. Well, you'll be relieved to know this version is waterproof, to a certain depth anyway."

She really liked it when he laughed. The corners of his eyes crinkled and he had a twinkle in his eye that showed he really meant it. She moved across to stand by him as he passed her the phone.

"Here you are," he said. "Longer battery life on this model, too."

"It's great. Thank you. I really appreciate it."

"It's the least I could do after what happened. I had them put additional antivirus and antiphishing software on the phone, too."

They set up her new phone and then had dinner together. Miles was good company and Chloe had to remind herself that she wasn't supposed to be enjoying him quite so much. One thing that did surprise her, as they kept their talk along very general lines, was that he never once mentioned his family. Then again, neither did she. It was as though, by some unspoken agreement, they'd decided not to discuss anything but the most peripheral of subjects. It was kind of refreshing, in a way.

After their meal, he helped her clean up and then she walked him out. For some reason, though, she felt awkward as she held the door open for him. She could see his car, the dark navy paintwork glinting under the streetlight, parked outside her house and the sheer luxury in every line of the vehicle reminded her of the gulf in their lives. Of him being a "have" and she having grown up a "have not." It firmed her resolve to see this through. She was scrambling to try to come up with a logical way to thank him for his help today and for his generosity with the phone and dinner, when he started to speak.

"I have tickets to a show in town tomorrow night."

He mentioned the name of an up-and-coming blues musician she'd been hoping to be able to hear perform live. "Would you be interested in coming with me?"

"Tomorrow? Wow, that would be great! Thank you. I'd love to go."

He grinned. "Awesome. I'll pick you up about seven. We can have a bite to eat before the show."

"Oh, it seems silly for you to come all the way out here to get me. I can meet you at the club if you'd rather."

"It's no bother. Besides, my mom would whip my butt if I expected my date to meet me at a function. She brought me up far better than that."

It was the first time he'd mentioned family. Interesting, she thought, that it had been his mom and not his dad who'd come up so casually in conversation.

"Well, then, I'd best let you make your mom proud."

He smiled. "Thank you. And thank you for tonight."

"Me? You brought dinner."

"Yeah, but you didn't have to share it with me."

"Oh? I didn't know that was an option. My mom always lived by the mantra that if you had more than you needed it was your obligation to share."

He winked at her. "She sounds like a wise woman."

"She can be."

She could also be bitter and trapped by circumstances. Circumstances created by the father of the man standing right there in front of her.

"Hey, we're all human, right?" Miles said. "I really enjoyed tonight."

"Me too," she murmured with genuine pleasure.

"I'm also glad you're happy to see me again."

And then he leaned in. Chloe's body, already wildly attuned to Miles, responded automatically,—closing the distance between them until his lips were on hers. In that instant, she lost all sense of where she was. All she could think about was the warm, firm pressure of his mouth on hers and how she'd been longing for it ever since that moment in the kitchen. Miles reached up with one hand and slid it under her hair to gently cup the back of her head. His fingertips against her scalp sent tiny zaps of electricity through her and she wondered what they would feel like on other, more sensitive, parts of her body.

She parted her lips slightly in invitation and Miles deepened the kiss. Her mind went into overload. The taste of him, the scent of his cologne, the gentle caress of his fingers, all of it combined to make her want to sink into him and lose herself completely.

And then, just like that, the kiss was over and he was pulling back. Releasing her. Giving her space.

"Wow," she said on a rush of air. "Do you kiss all the girls you knock over like that?"

"Only the ones I really, really like," he replied. This time his face was serious. Not even an ounce of humor colored his eyes, which had deepened to the bottomless green of a lake at twilight. "See you tomorrow."

He turned and walked down her front path and

she saw the interior light come on in his car as he unlocked it. He raised a hand briefly in farewell before getting in and driving away. Chloe closed and locked her front door and leaned against it, her fingertips on her lips, reliving the kiss they'd just shared.

She was playing with fire. She only hoped she wouldn't get burned.

Four

As he drove along the interstate toward the city, Miles couldn't help but savor the anticipation of seeing Chloe again. That kiss last night had knocked him sideways. He hadn't meant to kiss her just yet. In fact, he'd planned to make their first embrace something special, to be remembered for location and timing as well as for content. But need had overcome rationality and he wasn't a bit sorry about it.

He wanted to repeat the experience and this time he was going to ensure that it would be a moment to savor and that they wouldn't be framed in a well-lit doorway open to the street and any passersby. Miles pulled up outside Chloe's place and was halfway down the path when she came out the front door to greet him. He stopped in his tracks and let his eyes roam the loveliness that greeted him.

She'd gathered her fine blond hair up into a knot at the nape of her slender neck and delicate gold chain earrings hung from her earlobes. The dress she wore was black and beaded with fine black crystals and had a deep V-neck that exposed a great deal of lightly tanned skin. His eyes were drawn to the gentle swell of her breasts and the slight flush of color at her chest. Nerves, perhaps? Whatever it was, she was a vision and he felt a pulse of feral need beat in his veins at the sight of her.

"You look stunning," he said as he continued up the walk to meet her.

She ducked her head slightly before angling her neck and looking up at him.

"Thank you. Not too much? You didn't say where we were going and I've always been taught it's better to overdress than turn up looking like a slob."

He laughed. "You are nothing like a slob. This is perfect."

He looked at her again, noting the way the cocktail dress skimmed her hips and ended a few inches above her knees. Not so short as to cheapen the outfit, and not so long as to dampen desire. The dress looked as though it had been made for her. She wore heels that made her at least three inches taller, but he still topped her by inches. They'd make a very distinctive couple tonight, he thought as he offered her his arm.

"All locked up?"

She nodded and took his arm with her good hand.

"How's your wrist today?"

She held up the bandaged appendage. "Much better today, thanks."

"And the phone? It meets your needs?"

"Perfectly, thank you."

They were at the car and he reached for the door, holding it open for her as she lowered herself to the passenger seat and drew her legs in. He tried not to stare but the sight of those long, slender, bare legs sent another jolt of pure male appreciation spearing through his body. He wished he knew her well enough that he could suggest skipping the show tonight and cutting straight to dessert at his place instead. But he appreciated there was a process to follow when it came to courting.

Was he courting her? he wondered as he closed her door and walked around to the driver's side of the car. It was such an old-fashioned term. Certainly not one he'd ever considered in any of his previous relationships. But then again, he'd never felt about anyone the way he already felt about Chloe. The need to understand her and to share her thoughts and dreams had sneaked into his mind several times each hour of his working day. He'd always been able to compartmentalize before. Work life, personal life. They were two distinctly separate things. But when it came to this woman, everything was different.

By the time they reached the club, they'd covered every inane subject under the sun from Chicago's public transport system to the current state of public school education in Illinois. She was a passionate advocate for her kids, he noticed, and he envied her students in some ways. To be the recipient of her love of teaching combined with a keen interest in the world around her that he knew would light fires of curiosity in many of her students, would be a precious gift indeed.

Miles got out of the car at the valet parking station and went round to the other side. Chloe's door had already been opened for her and she was waiting on the sidewalk.

"I've heard about this place. Do you come here often?" she asked.

Miles nodded. "I love it. The atmosphere inside is second to none, and they always have great artists. We're ahead of most of the crowd. I considered taking you somewhere else for dinner but they do great meals here, too."

"Good," she answered as she took his arm and they carried on inside the building. "'Cause I'm starved."

"You look like you hardly eat at all," he teased. "Or did you just save all your appetite for me?"

She stumbled slightly and he steadied her. She looked him square in the eye. "Oh, I've saved my appetite. I've learned never to let opportunity pass me by."

Miles couldn't help but wonder at the double entendre in her words.

"Is that what I am? An *opportunity*?" he probed.

"Well, that remains to be seen, doesn't it?" she replied coyly.

Miles decided to shelve that train of thought for another time as the hostess came forward to greet them. She showed them to a cozy, private table for two, which also had a great view of the stage.

"Can I get you both a drink before I send your waiter across with menus?" the woman asked.

"Sure, I'm in the mood to celebrate," Miles said, turning toward Chloe. "How about you? Champagne to mark our first date?"

A huge smile spread across her face. "Champagne? Really? We might hate each other by the end of the night."

"Somehow, I doubt that. Besides, I've learned that you have to take time to stop and celebrate every facet of life. I think tonight is a good place to start."

He'd surprised her. Again. She thought she'd done her background search on him quite thoroughly, but he continued to deviate from the type of character she thought he really was. She decided it was time to probe a little deeper.

After their champagne had been brought and poured, Miles handed her a glass, then held up his in tribute.

"To you," he said simply.

Chloe felt a blush rise on her cheeks and bent her head in acknowledgment. No one had ever toasted her before. Not when she'd graduated college, not when she'd secured her first permanent teaching position—never. It was quite a rush, she decided, having someone appreciate you so openly. She took a sip of the golden, sparkling liquid in her glass and enjoyed the fizz on her tongue as she swallowed a mouthful. Oh yes. She could get used to this. But then again, wouldn't she have been used to this if it hadn't been for the Wingate family in the first place?

She wondered when the last time was that her mother had enjoyed something as simple as a glass of imported wine. In fact, when was the last time her mother had enjoyed anything? Chloe racked her brain and was shocked to discover that she barely remembered the last time she'd seen her mother smile, let alone laugh or simply bask in the joy of a sunny day. Loretta Fitzgerald's entire life had become a bitter circle of distrust and regret. Which was precisely why Chloe was even here in the first place. She wasn't supposed to be enjoying herself, and yet she couldn't help but relish the attention Miles showed her, or the way he could coax a chuckle from her when she least expected it.

"Why so pensive?" he asked. "We're celebrating, remember?"

"Oh, family stuff. You know what it's like."

Oh no, she thought. Had she just let slip that she knew more about his family than she ought to know?

"Families. Can't live with 'em, can't live without 'em," he said with a tone of inevitability she hadn't heard from him before. "I chose to move away from mine. It was too hard trying to always live up to expectations that were unreasonable and didn't take into account my own dreams for the future. I guess that makes me the black sheep of my lot."

"Your lot? You have brothers and sisters?" she pressed, even though she knew the answer.

"Two of each, for my sins," he said with a rueful smile. "And a couple of cousins who are like brothers to me as well."

"Wow," Chloe remarked, putting her glass down carefully on the table in front of her. She didn't want to drink too much and potentially put her foot into what were undoubtedly treacherous waters. "I can't imagine being part of a large family like that. Were you close as youngsters?"

Miles shrugged. "When my father wasn't trying to pit us all against one another. Dad was a man driven to succeed, at any cost."

Yes, even at the cost of another man's life, Chloe thought bitterly.

"That must have been hard on all of you. Did your mom make up for that?"

"It had its moments," he said sparingly. "And, actually, Mom isn't too different. She's always been driven to succeed and expected the same of all of us. Not the most maternal type."

He cleared his throat, then went on. "Anyway, after college, I moved to Chicago to make my own way. And I have. Dad died a couple of years back. He never told me that he was proud of what I'd achieved. It wasn't until after he'd gone that I realized how important that was to me, to actually hear him say the words. Now I've decided that his opinion doesn't matter. I'm here for me. To live my best life. It's why I go for what I want when I see it and I make no apology for that."

"And why should you. Isn't that how we should all live? Striving for what we want? Honestly, as long we don't do harm to others, isn't that the way to live our best lives?"

Miles cocked his head and looked at her carefully. "I'm more and more convinced that fate put you on that collision course with me yesterday. Does that sound corny?"

Oh, it was *fate* all right. A fate that had begun with his father's ill treatment of hers. She tamped down the bright flare of hurt and anger that burned inside her and painted a smile on her face.

"Maybe it would to anyone else, but it doesn't to me."

Of course it didn't sound corny to her, because she'd orchestrated their meeting so carefully. She'd plotted and planned and it had almost gone awry. But out of nothing had come this growing connection with Miles Wingate. He was not the man she'd thought he was. After reading all the articles that had talked about how hardheaded he was and how successful his security business had become—she'd tarred him with his father's brush. Chloe knew that success always came at a cost. Was she prepared to pay the price for hers?

She was powerfully drawn to Miles. It was there in the way her heart raced when she saw him. It was there in the way her body reacted with the age-old pull of desire that drew her insides into a knot at his touch. And that kiss of his? Well, that had stimulated a long-dormant libido that had sent her subconscious into overdrive during last night's sleep.

If their circumstances had been different, she'd be able to allow herself to enjoy his company more. She wouldn't have to remain on tenterhooks all the time, wondering if she was going to say or do something that might reveal her true intentions. And what were those exactly? She asked herself the question simply to remind herself to remain on track.

She wanted the entire Wingate family to feel the shame she'd been forced to grow up with. It had started already in the media, with the family's jewel in the crown, WinJet—their private jet manufacturing company—in the headlines for all the wrong reasons. The scandal would be hurting them, even Miles. They were, historically, a family that couldn't bear to be seen to be less than perfect. But the cracks were beginning to show, and when she uncovered new information about the family to give to the reporter and he took it—and her father's story—public, that would blow those cracks wide-open.

Revealing that the patriarch of the Wingate family had driven a business colleague to suicide, then swept in and bought up what was left of that friend's company in order to consolidate WinJet's early entry into the aviation industry, would confirm to all the world that the recent incident at the WinJet plant was merely proof that the rot in the family and their companies was systemic.

"You're not drinking your champagne. Is it not to your taste?" Miles asked, interrupting her reveries.

"It's delicious. I just want to make it last so I can enjoy it longer."

"I can make sure you enjoy it all night long. Just say the word."

Chloe was saved from saying the word that hovered on the edge of her lips by the arrival of a waiter with menus. She took her time poring over the available selections. Her mind was so scattered by Miles's comment, and her own willingness to say a categorical "yes" to whatever he suggested, that she had to get herself back under control. None of this was turning out how she expected it to.

She sighed. Wearing the vintage cocktail dress she'd picked up in a charity store near one of the more affluent suburbs in Chicago had been a calculated risk. He could have turned up in jeans and a T-shirt, geared up for a casual evening, but the moment she'd spied him through her living room window and seen the cut of his suit and the polish to his shoes, she'd known she'd done the right thing. The dress accentuated her good points and she'd seen the way he'd looked at her when she'd come out to greet him.

It did a woman's soul good to feel appreciated. And he'd made her soul sing. Not just when he arrived but when he'd made that toast, too. From any other man it might have come across as orchestrated or false, but from Miles it felt right on an entirely instinctive level. She was wildy attracted to him. From his short, dark blond hair and green-eyed gaze, to the way his large, masculine hands so capably did whatever he set out to do.

She looked at those hands now. Remembered the punch of awareness that had rippled through her at his touch. Sex with him would be incendiary. She knew it as well as she knew the sun rose each morning. That pulse of lust deep in her lower belly pulled stronger. She dragged her gaze from his hands. What the heck was she doing thinking about sex with a man who was virtually a stranger to her? A man who was part of a family she'd loathed and envied for nineteen years of her life.

Things aren't always as they seem.

One of her father's favorite sayings slid through from the back of her mind, prompting her to wonder why on earth she had thought of that right now. Was it that Miles was not as he seemed? Or maybe it was that he was exactly as he seemed and her perception of his family was the part that was tainted.

Chloe had heard that revenge could be a double-edged sword but she never expected the execution of that revenge would cause her so much confusion. The waiter returned for their orders and she dragged her thoughts back to the menu in her hands.

"Look, I'm hopeless when I'm given too many choices. What do you recommend?" she asked of the young man standing patiently beside her.

"The lobster is always good, ma'am," he said deferentially.

"Fine, I'll have the lobster."

"Make that two," Miles said. "If we're going to get messy, it may as well be together."

There he was again, with a comment that was perfectly innocent, and yet not at the same time. Chloe involuntarily pressed her thighs together, the movement increasing rather than relieving the demand building in her core.

And so the evening went. A little conversation, the sharing of the occasional anecdote from childhood, the mutual enjoyment of their meals and the champagne that accompanied it. By the time the band began to set up for the show, Chloe was feeling relaxed and happy. Two states she didn't usually indulge in.

She glanced across the small table at Miles, who was slightly sprawled on his chair and looking toward the stage.

"Thank you," she said with a depth of feeling that made him sit up straight and look at her with a question in his eyes and one brow raised. "Tonight is perfect."

Miles reached across the table and took her hand, his thumb brushing back and forth over her knuckles.

"Good. You deserve perfect."

Just like that, he stole her breath away and, she suspected, a piece of her heart as well. The band began to play and the featured artist began to sing a smooth, slow bluesy number that spread from her ears to her muscles, making her feel lissome and sensual and craving a fulfilment that she knew would only come with total capitulation to her desires. Miles continued to hold her hand throughout the performance. The slow touch of his thumb across her knuckles just made her want more of him touching more of her. By the time he tugged her to her feet and led her onto the tiny dance floor and drew her close, she was primed for anything.

Dancing with him was an exercise in restraint—and temptation all rolled into one. When he bent his head and whispered in her ear, she felt his warm breath on her skin and suddenly the music she'd been aching to hear all day was replaced with a deeper ache that she knew only this man could assuage.

"I like the feel of you in my arms," he said huskily.

She nuzzled the side of his neck and, suddenly emboldened, nipped the skin just beneath his ear.

"I like everything about you," she replied.

She felt the shock of his reaction shudder through him and he stopped moving. Another couple on the dance floor bumped into them, but he was oblivious to anything but her. She discovered that she really liked being the center of his universe. Even if it was only for this moment.

"Let's get out of here," Miles ground out.

"Yes."

Her response was short and sweet and thrilling all at the same time. Miles took her by the hand back to their table where she retrieved her evening bag and he went to settle their check. She met him by the front door. There was a fire burning in his eyes. Eyes which locked on her as she approached him.

He smiled at her and she felt her entire body react at the promise reflected there in his face.

She knew they'd only met yesterday. She knew that she had an ulterior motive. But right now all she could think about was how much she wanted him. *All* of him.

The valet had brought his car to the door and they drove in a tense kind of silence for what seemed to be a very short distance to his town house. She barely noticed the pretty facade to the three-story building and didn't, in fact, realize it was one house until they stepped through the ornate front door and into the spacious foyer and she saw the flights of stairs curving to the floors above.

"This is all yours?" she asked, looking around her at the quality furnishings and the high ceilings.

"Is that a problem?"

"No, not at all. It just seems like a lot of house for one person. That is, if you're living here alone."

Oh heck, she was messing everything up. The atmosphere that had enveloped them back at the club had cocooned them in a cloud of sensual promise. And now she was discussing his real estate?

"Yeah, it is. One day I hope to share it with a special someone and maybe fill it with kids, too."

A deep sense of longing threaded through his words, and she felt an answering tug from deep in her chest. Those were the things she wanted most, too. That special someone. A family of her own. Growing up as an only child hadn't been so bad, until her father had died. After that she'd been so afraid and felt so insecure. Having a sibling to share her feelings with would have meant the world to her. Instead, she'd had to be her mother's support person, which, at eight years old, had forced her to grow up way too fast.

Miles reached a hand for her and she slipped her palm in his. Instant warmth flooded her. She liked the way his fingers curled around hers, infusing her with his strength and purpose. He turned to the stairwell and she followed him as he ascended to the next floor. Then he led her down a thickly carpeted corridor to a room at the end where he pushed open the double doors and led her inside.

A large master suite spread before her. Heavy drapes hung in the tall windows overlooking the back of the property and a massive bed dominated the center of the room. She looked from the bed to Miles. There was an unspoken question in his eyes. In response, she turned in his arms and lifted her face to his.

He groaned in what she hoped was relief and then his lips were on hers and he kissed her, hard and deep and with a longing that mirrored her own. Sensation poured through her body as he wrapped his arms around her and held her close. The hard muscles of his chest pressed against the softness of her breasts, and she felt her nipples stiffen at the pressure. Deep in her lower belly, need throbbed with an insistent demand, and she pressed her pelvis against him, rocking gently and moaning into his mouth. She felt his hands searching for the zipper of her dress and forced herself to tear her mouth from his.

"It's on my left-hand side," she murmured before kissing him again.

His fingers found the zipper, and she felt the fabric loosen around her body before he lifted both hands to her shoulders and gently eased the fabric down her arms, taking care not to tug on her injured wrist. He eased the gown over her hips and let it drop in a pool at her feet. She hadn't worn a bra tonight and he gave a sharp intake of breath when he realized she was standing there dressed in nothing but a lace thong and a pair of high-heeled shoes that showcased her long lean legs to perfection.

"You're a dream come true," he said with a slow smile.

"And you're wearing entirely too many clothes," she replied, and reached up to help him off with his jacket.

Her fingers were a little clumsy as she reached for the buttons of his shirt and slowly slid each one from its buttonhole and yanked the tails from the waistband of his trousers. She pressed her palms against his bare chest and splayed her fingers over his muscles. Her wrist twinged at the movement, but she ignored it because for some weird reason, it felt as if by skin-to-skin contact he was sharing his energy with her and she ached to feel more of him.

Chloe placed a wet kiss at the base of his throat and then trailed a line of kisses to one of his nipples while her fingers traced a circle around the other.

Miles didn't remain a disinterested party. His hands were at her waist, then sliding up over her rib cage to cup her breasts. She wasn't heavily endowed in that area but he didn't appear to be complaining. And nor was she as ripples of delight spread through her as he gently cupped and squeezed her breasts and rolled her tightly budded nipples between his fingers.

He was still overdressed, she decided, and she reached for his belt buckle. Her hands shook a little as she undid it and then loosened the fastening at the top of his zipper before pulling his zipper down and pushing his pants down past his thighs. Formfitting boxer briefs wrapped around his hips, and there was no doubting he was as turned on as she was. She grasped his length through the stretch cotton, relishing the hardness and the heat of him.

Miles kissed her again before saying, "Let's move this to the bed, hmmm?"

Chloe stepped out of the glittering black circle of fabric pooled at her feet and walked across to the expansive bed, while Miles quickly divested himself of his shoes and socks and kicked his trousers to one side. He shrugged his shirt off, letting it fall on top of the rest of his clothing, and followed behind her. Then he reached past her to yank back the bedcovers and coax her onto the high thread count sheets that felt silken soft beneath her buttocks.

Miles knelt between her legs and removed her shoes, pressing a kiss into the arch of each of her feet as he did so. The sensation of his mouth against her incredibly sensitive skin sent spirals of pleasure up her legs and to the apex of her thighs. She was already wet for him, wet and ready and aching for his possession but he seemed to want to take his time. He trailed small kisses on the inside of her ankles, up along her calves, then the backs of her knees. She had no idea she had so many erogenous zones on her body, and she dropped back against the sheets, focusing solely on the pleasure he offered.

The feeling of his lightly stubbled jaw and the warm, wet heat of his mouth on her inner thighs made her moan again. And at her core she felt an insistent, pounding demand for more. His lips and hands drew inexorably closer to her center, and when his mouth closed over her and he pushed a warm breath through the lace of her thong she felt her hips lift off the bed in a desperate involuntary thrust.

She felt his fingers at the edges of her thong, and she fought the urge to beg him to move faster.

"You like that?" Miles rasped.

"Oh yes, please don't stop."

"What about this?" he asked as he brushed a finger around the entrance to her body, coating it in her moisture before encircling her clit.

"Yes! That, too."

He kept up the motion, pressing incrementally more firmly and driving her closer and closer to climax.

"I think we can get rid of these now, don't you?" he said and withdrew his hand to ease her thong down her legs and off completely.

She felt totally exposed, lying there with her legs

splayed, but there was no embarrassment or discomfort. Instead she was mesmerized by the look on his face as he gazed down on her.

"You are so beautiful, Chloe. I want to give you so much pleasure you can barely think."

She wanted that, too. "Yes," she whispered, incapable of saying more.

He traced the inner edges of her hips and his fingers trailed down, down, down to her aching center. And then he bent his head and pressed his mouth to her clitoris, his tongue sweeping against the sensitive bud in a firm rhythmic motion, driving her absolutely wild. He slid a finger inside her body, murmuring in appreciation as she clenched around him. The stroking of his tongue combined with his deep, probing touch pushed her even higher until, in a rushing crescendo of pleasure, she tumbled off the peak of anticipation and into a breathless maelstrom of marvel as pulse after pulse of pleasure racked her.

Her entire body continued to tremble as her climax slowly faded, leaving her limp and sated at the same time. Miles rose to his feet, lifted her from the edge of the bed and lay her fully onto the middle of the mattress before he slipped off his briefs and joined her. The heat of his strong body alongside hers was searing, and Chloe could feel his erection against her hip. She reached for him, stroking the silken skin of his shaft all the way to the tip and then back down again.

"If you keep that up, things are going to get intense around here," he rumbled in her ear.

"Intense? I think I like intense. Don't you?"

"Oh yeah."

Chloe forced herself to move and straddled him in a lithe movement. Her entire body still felt sensitized by the heady satisfaction he'd given her. Now it was his turn.

"Condom?" she asked.

"Top drawer of the nightstand."

She reached over, letting her breasts brush against his naked torso as she did so, and retrieved a strip of condoms from the drawer. She held the strip up in front of her as she settled back down over his thighs.

"Hmm, impressive," she teased. "Good to see you're prepared."

His eyes glittering, he looked up at her and chuckled.

"You don't find that intimidating?"

She smiled in return. "Not at all. I'm a girl who enjoys a challenge. Let's see how many of these you have left by morning."

Chloe quickly tore a packet open and sheathed him before lifting her body higher and positioning herself over his erection. She slowly lowered herself, taking him deeper and deeper. The sensation of his shaft against her still-tingling and sensitive core made her insides clench and she relished the sound of his groan as she tightened around him. Miles slid his hands along her thighs and up to her hips. She tilted her pelvis so his length slid a little deeper and rocked there.

"Oh, you're a torment," he said on a harshly blown out breath.

"You haven't seen anything yet," she crooned, then proceeded to show him exactly what she meant.

By the time he was shuddering into his own climax, Chloe was a beat away from another spine-tingling orgasm, and as she gave herself over to the sheer joy of it and collapsed against his body in paroxysms of delight, she knew that as far as Miles Wingate was concerned, revenge was the last thing on her mind.

Five

Physically, he was exhausted, and yet he'd never felt more energized in his life. Miles turned his head on the pillow and looked at the woman responsible for his current state. Blond hair tangled against the pillowcase and a sweep of lashes lay on her flushed cheeks as she slept deeply. *And so she ought to*, he thought. They'd spent the better part of the night discovering exactly what brought one another pleasure and, since there was only one condom left, he'd have to make another trip to the drugstore, he noted with a wicked grin.

"What are you smiling about?" she asked with one blue eye open.

"Your willingness to take on a challenge," he answered, rolling onto his side so he could better appreciate the view of her naked body.

The top sheet and comforter had hit the floor somewhere around 4:00 a.m. and the warm glow of the morning sunshine gilded her skin like a lover's caress. Like *his* caress, he realized. They'd become lovers in every sense of the word last night. And here she was, still in his bed. No sneaky dawn exit. No regrets. Nothing but a sense of well-being he'd never known before.

He'd thought she was special from the moment they'd met, and he hadn't wanted to leave her to her own devices. But during the night he'd begun to grasp just how special she truly was. He'd heard of people embarking on whirlwind romances before, but he'd never thought it would happen to him. He was far too focused, too pragmatic to fall for flights of fancy. So if this wasn't a romantic whim, what was it?

"Well, I think even I have hit my limit when it comes to challenges," she said on a yawn.

"It's always good to know your limits," he drawled, tracing a finger over the delicate curve of her shoulder and down her arm. "How's your wrist today?"

"A bit achy to be honest."

"Then let me take care of you."

And he did, slowly, deliberately and carefully as if he was making love to a figurine made of spun glass. There was something to be said for fast and frenzied, but then again taking it slow made everything all the more poignant and special. Every breath shared, every touch, every ripple of sensation through their bodies was experienced a thousandfold times deeper—as if they were making love on an emotional level as well as the physical. As if they were irrevocably bonding together in a way he'd never known with another.

When their climaxes came, they were in total sync. And instead of the intense rocket of satisfaction that was normal for him, he felt his pleasure spread through his entire body, growing stronger and deeper with each beat of his heart before ending on a starburst of sensation that almost brought tears to his eyes. He spied a telltale trail of moisture leaking from the corners of Chloe's eyes and knew it had been equally special for her. Gathering her into his arms, he rolled them both onto their sides as they waited for their heart rates to return to normal.

"Spend the day with me," he said.

Oh sure, he knew he should have phrased it as a question—that would have been the polite thing to do—but it would have given her a choice.

And he couldn't bear the thought of her saying no.

"I don't have any clothes, or are you suggesting I won't need any?"

He laughed. He really loved the way Chloe responded to him. Then he realized, in her own way, she'd acquiesced to his demand and a burst of sheer joy ballooned in his chest.

"We can go back to your place. Maybe you could pack a bag. Stay the whole weekend with me?"

This time he made it sound like a question and it wasn't until she nodded and said yes that he realized just how much he'd hoped for her affirmative answer.

"Why don't you go shower. There's a robe behind the bathroom door you can borrow. I'll make us some breakfast and then we can head out to your place."

"Sounds good. You don't want to join me in the shower?"

"I have the feeling that if I do we might both not be capable of walking afterward," he said with a grin. "Besides, we're out of condoms."

She laughed and got out of the bed. "There are other options," she murmured slyly.

Despite having just made love to her, Miles felt his libido begin to stir to life again.

"Tempting, but I'm starving. Food first, then clothes, then other options," he said.

"Sounds good to me."

He watched her as she crossed the bedroom and went into the en suite bathroom. Every cell in his body urged him to follow her, but he overrode the impulse and got up, pulling on a pair of sweatpants and a T-shirt and heading downstairs to the kitchen. He'd just poured two glasses of juice and put beaten eggs in the pan to scramble when Chloe entered the kitchen dressed in his robe.

Seeing her in his clothing gave him a sucker punch to the chest and a sense of pride he never imagined he was capable of feeling.

"You were quick in the shower," he commented as he forced his attention back to the eggs.

"My mom was very much into saving while I was growing up. I learned to be frugal in everything, including my showers."

Miles let her words sink in. He'd had no such boundaries placed on his life as a child. There was always an abundance of everything. If you were hungry, you went to the kitchen, and Martha, their cook, would always find you something. If you were thirsty, you helped yourself to a drink. If you wanted a shower, there was no one beating on your door to hurry up because in their home there were more bathrooms than bedrooms. He had no response for Chloe because he could not fathom what her life must have been like.

She sat on one of the stools at the kitchen's central island.

"Scrambled eggs! Yum. My favorite kind of breakfast."

At the end of the counter, the toaster popped.

"I hope you like toast with your eggs?"

"Sure, would you like me to butter it?"

"Yep, butter is in the fridge. Plates are warming in the oven"

She went and retrieved the toast, buttered it and put the slices on the two plates in the oven.

"I wasn't sure if you preferred tea or coffee at breakfast, but I have poured you juice."

"I'm a tea in the morning kind of girl. I can make it."

He told her where to the find the tea and cups and watched her as she moved confidently around the kitchen. He liked having her here, working along-side him. And it made him look forward to the rest of the day and the weekend following that they had before them. He plated up the eggs and put the plates at the place settings he'd made on the kitchen island, then poured himself a coffee before joining Chloe.

"This looks great, thanks," she said, tucking straight into the creamy scrambled eggs. "Mmm, and it tastes great, too. What kind of herb did you use?"

"Dill," he replied. "I wasn't sure if you'd like it but eggs are so plain without embellishment."

"I haven't tried it before but I really like it. What made you become so adept in the kitchen?"

He took a mouthful of his own eggs and chewed and swallowed before answering. "I used to watch our cook, Martha, a lot. She would always give a run-ning commentary while she was cooking, whether anyone was listening or not. I am lucky enough that I have a very good auditory memory and I picked up most of my cooking skills from her. The rest I've learned along the way. Living on your own, it's a challenge to keep things interesting when it comes to food, don't you think?"

"Yes and no. I've been lucky enough to have a roommate most of the time. You haven't had anyone living with you here?"

He heard the probing note in her voice. The ques-tion about whether he'd lived with another woman hanging on the air—there, yet not quite verbalized.

"I've had this place for five years and, no, I've

never had a roommate or any other kind of mate stay here before."

"You mean stay, or move in? Oh heck, I'm sorry. I shouldn't be so darn nosy. It always gets me into trouble. You don't have to answer that."

Her cheeks had flushed a charming shade of pink and she refused to meet his gaze, finding refuge in lifting her cup of tea and taking a great big swig of the liquid instead.

"I'll answer it because I think it deserves to be said. No, I've never had anyone stay over before, or move in."

Silence stretched between them. Eventually Chloe replaced her cup in its saucer and faced him.

"So I'm your first?"

"So to speak, yes."

She let out a long breath. "Wow. Thank you, I think."

"No need to thank me. I always knew the right person would come along at the right time. I just never expected that to be on the path at Lincoln Park, is all."

She laughed but he could sense a restraint in her that wasn't there before. Miles reached out and took her hand in his.

"No pressure, Chloe. We can take this at your pace. You can even tell me you never want to see me again. I'll accept it. Not happily, but I will survive. But I think that what we have is something special. Something worth exploring. I feel like I have a connection to you." He shook his head. "Listen to me,

I sound like something out of a romantic movie. I don't want this to come across as clichéd, but I mean what I said. And I hope you still want to spend the next few days with me."

This was the time to do it. The time she needed to come clean and tell Miles exactly why they'd bumped into one another. The thing was, she didn't want to destroy this incredibly special and potentially fragile thing they had going. It was clear he had nothing to do with the Wingate fortune and, from what she'd seen so far, little to do with his family, either. They didn't come up in general conversation in the way of people who actually spent time in their siblings' company. So, even if she did tell him, would that damage what they had going?

She stared into Miles's intense green eyes and asked herself if she could risk shattering their fledgling relationship, and the answer was a resounding no. He was different than any other man she'd ever dated. And he wanted her. *Really* wanted her. That was a feeling she'd never experienced before. Most of the other men she'd gone out with had always kept themselves aloof, except if they'd wanted sex.

Maybe part of that had been her fault. Choosing men who were commitment-shy because deep down Chloe was afraid to trust completely, or to give herself to another without restraint. Losing her dad and seeing how his death had affected her mom had left deep emotional scars. Loving someone so completely was scary. There had always been something lacking in her previous relationships—whether it was her partners' fault, or her own. But now, even after this impossibly short time, she knew exactly what that something was. Intimacy and commitment. And Miles appeared to be prepared to give both those things to her.

"Don't think you can scare me away so easily," Chloe said, deliberately keeping her tone light even though what they were discussing was 100 percent serious. "I absolutely want to spend today and the weekend with you. And I hope our friendship won't stop there, Miles. Besides, who else is going to cook me eggs like these?"

She saw him visibly relax and realized, with some relief, that she'd struck just the right note.

"Well, aside from Martha, who retired several years ago and who lives in Texas, there isn't anyone who can cook eggs just like these, so it looks like we're stuck with each other. In the best possible way, of course."

She couldn't help the grin that spread across her face. She really liked how he spoke seriously one minute, then resorted to humor the next. This was going to be a very provocative weekend. But, it occurred to her, today was only Friday.

"Don't you have work today?"

He shrugged. "One of the perks of being the head honcho. I can delegate, and I did. I rang my office while you were in the shower. They'll manage just fine without me for a day. I want to give you my full attention, get to know you better. You know, the usual stuff people do when they like each other."

Like? She had no doubt she was in danger of more than liking him. And she suspected he felt the same way. The novelty of that was incredibly refreshing.

"That sounds like fun. I'd like that. Have you thought about what we might do today, aside from pick up a change of clothing for me, that is?"

She plucked at the lapels of his robe. When she'd put it on she'd caught the faint whiff of his cologne and it had done crazy things to her insides. She had felt like a giddy schoolgirl wearing her boyfriend's sweater for the very first time. It was ridiculous, really, and yet it had left her feeling as if her blood fizzed in her veins. She was looking forward to spending time with him far more than she'd anticipated.

"I thought we could go for a stroll around the aquarium then maybe head to Navy Pier? You up for that?"

"Fish followed by carnival rides? You bet!"

"So, did you want to think about that a little?" he teased with a laugh.

"Absolutely not. I hardly ever got to do things like that as a kid, so you can be sure I'll make the most of the day. How about I clean up here in the kitchen while you shower and get dressed. Then we can get started."

"Yes, ma'am," Miles answered. He leaned over and kissed her briefly on the mouth. "I really like your enthusiasm, but you're really bad for my work ethic. That's twice now this week I've played hooky to be with you."

She felt a dip in her tummy. "Is that okay? I mean, you said you're the boss and all, but can you afford to be away from work this much?"

He kissed her again. "Don't worry. I have an excellent team working for me. Sometimes I feel quite redundant around the place."

"Okay, then. If you're sure."

"I'm sure," he confirmed.

"Fine. Now hurry up and get ready so we can go and have some fun."

Miles rushed through his shower and got dressed. When he came out of the bathroom, he noticed that Chloe had already made the bed and picked up her clothing from last night. The girl moved fast, he thought, with approval. In fact, he liked the way she moved, period.

She was downstairs waiting for him in the foyer, dressed in her cocktail dress and heels again. He felt that now-familiar tug of attraction when he saw her. Man, it didn't matter if she was dressed to the nines or simply wearing his robe and fresh from a shower. The magnetic pull between them did not abate in any way.

"I feel strangely underdressed," he said, gesturing to his T-shirt and chinos.

"You look perfect," she replied, then blushed.

He cocked his head and looked at her. "Perfect, huh? You're good for my ego."

She laughed out loud. "Somehow I don't think your ego needs a lot of boosting."

He pulled a face. "Are you saying I'm conceited?"

"No, in fact, with someone with your level of privilege, you're refreshingly unpretentious."

He studied her again. "My level of privilege?"

She waved her hand to encompass the lavish entrance of his home. "Need I say more?"

"Okay, you made your point. Let's go get you into something more suited to a day out with an unpretentious man of privilege."

"Are you going to tease me about that all day?"

"No, I'm sure I'll find something else to tease you about," he said lightheartedly.

But her comment had stung just a little. He'd grown up in a family with immense wealth and privilege and a father whose sense of entitlement had made him a difficult man at the best of times. Miles had done everything he could, his entire adult life, not to become the man his father was. But did a man have to live in a hovel and dress like a pauper to make his point? Miles had never thought so. Yes, he was wealthy, but he'd earned that wealth based on sound business decisions and his own intelligence. And he'd held on to it and continued to build it in the same way.

As he and Chloe drove out to Midlothian, he wondered what had prompted her remark. Obviously she'd been burned somewhere along the line. But how badly, and would it make an impact on their chances of building a future relationship?

And was he putting the cart before the horse by overthinking this entire thing? They'd only just met two days ago, after all, and they'd been more intimate in that time than he'd been in any of his past three relationships. He'd brought her home, and he never did that. He'd always wanted an out, in the past. But with Chloe, he just quite simply wanted *her*.

He reached across and grabbed her good hand and gave it a squeeze. Out of the corner of his eye he saw her look up at him and smile. He smiled back, realizing he'd probably laughed and smiled more in the past forty-eight hours than he had in the past forty-eight days.

Yeah, he wanted her, and sure, they might not be financial equals, but he had no doubt that when it came to the things that were important to him, like honesty for example, he and Chloe were very much on the same page.

Six

He really needed to take time off more often, Miles realized as they left the aquarium and headed to the pier. Chloe had exhibited a genuine delight in all they'd seen so far, and he found her enthusiasm infectious. He couldn't remember the last time he'd really relaxed and simply been in the moment like this. And sneaking kisses when she wasn't expecting them was fun, too.

However, walking around in a state of semiarousal all the time was something to get used to. Especially if he was planning to spend more time with Chloe. When they'd arrived at her house, she'd suggested he come in with her while she packed her bag for the weekend so he could advise her on wardrobe selections. Of course, being in her bedroom with her like that—well, one thing had led to another, and while he hadn't yet replenished his supply of condoms, it turned out that Chloe had a healthy supply of her own. Less one, now, he thought with a deep sense of satisfaction.

When they reached the pier, she dragged him onto the Ferris wheel. They were stalled at the top while people loaded in a car at the bottom, when he felt his phone vibrate in his pocket. He'd already told work, no calls unless it was a life-or-death situation—and in their line of work with clients all over the world in difficult circumstances, that could actually happen.

He slid his phone from his pocket and checked the screen. Sebastian? The elder of his twin brothers rarely called, but in light of the news reports about WinJet failing their safety inspection, hard on the heels of the news they were being sued by employees hurt in the recent fire at the plant, Miles knew this had to be important.

"I'm sorry, I'm going to have to take this," Miles said to Chloe.

"No problem," she replied breezily. "I'll just remain enraptured by the view."

She gave him a look that went from head to toe and back again, and Miles couldn't help the pull of attraction that flared under her gaze. He answered the call.

"Sebastian, what can I do for you?"

"What? No hello, brother, long time no see?"

There was an edge to his brother's voice that confirmed to Miles that this was definitely not a social call.

"I've seen the news. I assume that's why you're calling?"

Miles was careful to keep his choice of words as vague as possible. While there was little chance of being overhead way up here on the Ferris wheel, he wasn't about to take any unnecessary risks, either. Through the phone, he heard his brother sigh heavily.

"I wish I was calling under better circumstances."

His lips firmed into a straight line and he waited for his brother to continue.

"Look, Sutton and I have been talking. Something's not right about the whole situation, and we need someone with very specific expertise to make sure that the rot hasn't spread to our other companies."

"Expertise such as?"

"Someone we trust implicitly who is capable of doing a full forensic sweep of our systems. You're probably aware that we're being charged with criminal negligence in the jet plant fire, which our legal team is working on now. But it gets worse."

"Worse?"

Sebastian sighed again. "Look, I'll cut straight to the chase. During the independent safety inspection, drugs were found on the WinJet premises."

"*What?* Like a personal stash?"

"More like a considerable quantity for supply and distribution. The DEA have been brought in and they've opened an investigation. I can't tell you how serious this is. Based on their findings, they could have a case to present against us for drug trafficking."

Miles felt as if he'd been dealt a physical blow. A string of curse words escaped his mouth, and Chloe looked at him in concern. He reached for her hand and gave it a reassuring squeeze before thinking carefully about his reply to his brother.

"And, of course, you guys knew nothing about it, right?"

"Of course not." Sebastian sounded deeply insulted. "Look, you might not want to be a part of this family in a commercial sense, but I'd like to remind you that dirt sticks. If we're going to be tarred with this brush, it will affect you, too."

"I'm aware of that, and I know that you'd never dream of going down that road so don't get on your high horse with me, okay?" Miles fought the urge to lay a few more truths at his brother's door. Things like better IT security and plant surveillance, just to name a few, but that would be akin to locking the stable door after their entire breeding stock of horses on the ranch had bolted. "What do you want from me?"

"Can you come home? We'll give you access to all systems. Look, with the fire, everything is in disarray but one thing has become very clear since the investigation. Corners have been cut, and Sutton and I think it has to be someone at a higher level who authorized or instigated it. That someone has to have left a trail somewhere. We need you to find it."

Miles tried not to allow emotion to rule over common sense, but hearing his older brother tell him they needed him—well, it was hard to remain dispassionate after a comment like that.

"When?" he asked.

"Ideally? As soon as possible. We can send one of the company jets to collect you today. Can you be ready in about four hours?"

He could, but that would mean leaving Chloe behind on what was supposed to be a weekend getting to know one another. Of course, she'd be there when he returned, but now that she was with him, he didn't want to leave her. But the pull of family was strong, no matter how much he tried to pretend otherwise, and what his family was going through right now was deadly serious with far-reaching ramifications.

"Look, let me confirm with you in about an hour or so. There's something I need to take care of first."

"Something?" his brother asked wryly. "Or someone?"

And there it was, the usual big brother banter.

"I'll call you back," Miles said, deliberately ignoring Sebastian's question.

"I'll be waiting."

Miles disconnected and shoved his phone back in his pocket. Chloe was watching him carefully.

"Miles? Are you okay? You look like you've had a shock."

Yeah, he had received a shock. Hearing that the DEA were potentially preparing a case against his family for drug trafficking was hellishly serious.

"Family stuff," he gritted out without really saying anything at all. The car they were in on the Ferris wheel was nearing the exit point. "C'mon, let's go somewhere where we can talk."

Holding her hand, they exited the car, and Miles moved them through the crowd until they found a quiet spot on the edge of the pier.

"Chloe, I'm sorry, but our weekend plans are going to have to be put on hold."

"Of course, if your family needs you then they take precedence."

He felt the knot in his stomach begin to ease. He wasn't sure why he'd thought she'd object to the change in their plans. Maybe it was because the women in his experience to date, his mother and eldest sister included, had been the kind who disliked last minute changes in plans. Not that his mom or sister were princesses, far from it. They were sharp, intelligent and insightful women in their own right, but they also liked things their way.

"Thank you for understanding."

Chloe studied Miles's face carefully. He definitely looked conflicted by the news disclosed in the phone call. With the sounds of the pier and the music playing on the Ferris wheel, she hadn't been able to make out much of the conversation the two men had shared, but she'd seen the change in Miles's body language and his face had grown strained and serious. It still was.

She wondered what on earth had happened in the Wingate family that was so dire. That it had to do with the fire at WinJet was most likely. But even with the safety investigation and the bad publicity, they had more than enough money to make a payout to the injured parties and to ride out the storm until things settled down again. So what else could it be?

Chloe was suddenly reminded of her original plan with Miles Wingate. To get close, to find out secrets if she could, then to expose his family for the dirty, low-down scum they really were. She'd been distracted by the powerful physical attraction between her and Miles. Maybe this was the reminder she needed to get back on track and focus on the revenge she'd been planning for all her adult life. The revenge that she hoped would return her mother to being the woman she'd been back when Chloe's dad was still alive.

Dare she ask Miles what was involved in this sudden change to their plans? Of course she dared.

"What's wrong? Is there anything I can do to help you?"

He gave her a quick grin, but she noticed it didn't reach his eyes. Whatever this was, it had really done a number on him.

"This is something I need to take care of personally."

"Oh, secret squirrel stuff?"

That got a laugh out of him.

"Yeah, something like that. One of the family businesses had an accident. There's been an investigation into the cause, etc., but they need me to go deeper."

"Not something you can delegate, then?"

"Unfortunately, no. I'm really sorry, Chloe. I'm going to have to head to Texas later today."

"So soon?" She couldn't help the exclamation from spilling out. "Do you know how long you'll be away?"

"No. While that's not a problem for me with my business, it is a problem for us."

An idea came to mind. "It doesn't have to be."

"What do you mean?"

"Well, I'm still on summer break. Maybe I could come with you?" She deliberately hesitated a moment. "If you want me to, that is. Of course, I understand if you think I'm being ridiculous. After all we've only just met and—"

Miles kissed her into silence.

"That's the best idea I've heard all day! After all, you're already packed, right? We'd only need to stop by my place and then head out to the airfield. My brother said he'd send a plane. I just need to tell him when we'd be ready."

Chloe didn't know whether to sing for joy that her suggestion had been so willingly picked up, or to regret the rashness of it. Now it was out there, she needed to work with it.

"I'll need to make a few arrangements before we go," she told him. "Get my mail collected and someone in to water my plants. You know, the usual stuff. If you could run me back home, I could set all that up, add a few more things to my suitcase, then I can get a cab to the airport to meet you."

He nodded. "I'll tell Sebastian to send the plane

to Midway. But I won't hear of you taking a cab. I'll wait for you to get your things ready. I'll get my assistant to pack for me and meet us at the airport."

She wasn't about to argue, not when he'd accepted her suggestion so willingly.

Miles looked around them. "It seems a shame to have to leave all this."

"What, screaming kids, tired parents and too much cotton candy?"

"Well, when you put it that way?" He smiled and grabbed her hand, lifting it to his lips, where he pressed a kiss against her knuckles.

Chloe felt it all the way to the center of her body. The sounds around them almost faded completely away as her every cell focused solely on this man and his gentle touch. A pang of regret shafted through her as she reminded herself that this was all supposed to be fake. That she was seeking retribution and the peace it would hopefully bring her mother—not for her own gratification and, while she would have loved to have remained connected to him this way forever, she forced herself to pull free of his touch.

"Come on then, let's go. The sooner you call your brother, the sooner we can be on the road—or, as the case may be, in the air."

They made their way back to where Miles had parked his car and then drove to her house. He called his brother using the Bluetooth feature in his car. Once they arrived at Chloe's place, she went to her bedroom to phone her mother, while Miles called his assistant from the living room.

Loretta Fitzgerald answered on the third ring.

"Hi, Momma, how are you?" she asked brightly.

"Oh, you know. The usual. Yesterday would have been your dad's and my wedding anniversary. Those milestones are always tough."

Chloe felt a burning shame fill her. How could she have forgotten such an important date? Since her father's death, her mom had marked every milestone without him. Not with joy or happy memories, however. Most likely her mom had barely moved from her bed or opened her drapes. Her depression was mostly managed well, but anniversaries were particularly hard for her. If there was ever a day when her mom had needed her, it had been yesterday. And where had Chloe been? Wrapped up in Miles Wingate.

But then again, she rationalized, maybe knowing that her daughter was stepping up her goal of revenge against the Wingate family would make her mom feel as if they were finally getting closer to gaining closure on the Wingate family's responsibility behind her father's death.

"Momma, I'm sorry. I genuinely forgot."

"Oh, it's okay, hon. I know you can't buoy me along every day. You have your life to live."

It wasn't even as if her mom was being passive-aggressive. She honestly expected nothing in her life because she'd schooled herself to believe that if she expected nothing, she'd never be disappointed again.

"We both have our lives to live, Momma. And I have news. You know how we've often talked about making the Wingates pay for what they did to Daddy? Well, I met Miles Wingate the other day and, surprisingly, we've quickly become quite close."

"Oh, honey. I hope you know what you're doing. They might smile and look nice on the outside, but deep down they're like a viper's nest."

"I'm being careful," Chloe reassured her with the fingers of one hand firmly crossed. "Really careful, I promise. I won't get hurt. But I need to tell you that I'm going to be away for a few days. I'm going back to Texas, with Miles."

"Are you sure that's wise? Someone might recognize you. In fact, I'm surprised Miles didn't recognize you. We did mingle with the family on occasion back then."

"Not often enough for any memory of me to stick, I'm sure. And I'm all grown-up now. Nothing like the scrawny tomboy who was more interested in riding horses and climbing trees than in petit fours and lemonade on the veranda."

"You still miss your pony, don't you?" her mom said softly.

Chloe felt the all-too-familiar clutch in her chest when she thought about Trigger. He'd been one of the first things she'd truly loved that they'd had to let go after her father's death.

"I've moved on, Momma," Chloe lied. "And we'll both be able to move on once I've exposed their father for his part in Daddy's death."

"Well, if you're sure you're doing the right thing…"

Loretta didn't sound sure at all that her daughter was doing the right thing but, Chloe noted, she didn't tell her not to stay the course, either.

"I definitely am, Momma. We've discussed this. You know Daddy deserved better."

"I do, honey." A more positive note began to creep into Loretta's voice. "And he'd be so proud of you, too. It won't be easy going back. So many memories."

"Well, less for me than for you, I'm sure, Momma. And don't worry, I'll do you both proud. I promise." Chloe could hear Miles moving about in the living room and hastened to end the call. "Look, would you be able to clear my mailbox and water my plants while I'm away? I'll call you when I can, okay? Keep your fingers crossed for me."

"Sure I will. It'll do me good to have a reason to leave the house, and I'll keep everything crossed for you, Chloe. I love you."

"I love you, too, Momma. Talk later."

She ended the call and quickly repacked her case, ensuring that she put in a few items that would do in case they had to attend any formal events, including the dress she'd worn last night to dinner. Under her mother's tutelage, she'd developed an eye for what best suited her figure, and shopping in charity stores nearest the more expensive suburbs of Chicago had given her some lovely pieces for special occasions.

"Chloe, I don't want to rush you, but we really need to get going," Miles called out from the living room.

"It's okay. I'm just about done."

She swept a few more toiletries into the bag and zipped it shut before wheeling it out of her room. She studied Miles's face. Lines of strain had become apparent at the corners of his eyes, and his mouth, which she'd been accustomed to seeing curved into a smile, was a straight line.

"Is everything okay?" she asked.

His features softened as she approached him.

"Sure, at least it will be once I'm back with my family."

His words felt like bullets to her heart. *Family.* At least he had one, which was more than she and her mother could say. She'd been worried that she was making the right decision to follow through on her plan for payback, but this had just sealed the deal. As much as she was deeply attracted to him, she needed to remind herself that it was purely physical and the magnetic pull between them was merely a means to an end.

Miles and the rest of his brothers and sisters took their position in life and their wealth for granted. Wealth that was created, in part, on the backbone of her father's hard work. After her father's business had begun to suffer financial hardship due to a client going bankrupt and not settling their accounts with him, Trent Wingate had offered his support. But the support had never been forthcoming. Instead, the man had simply sat back and waited until he could swoop in and take over her father's business completely at a steal of a price, thereby driving him to his death.

Her daddy had thought Trent Wingate was a good man—someone he could count on—but his judgment had been fatally wrong. Chloe uttered a silent vow that she would not forget just how callous and cruel the Wingates could be. They needed a mirror brought before them to see how their choices and behaviors affected others. She would be that mirror, and maybe, just maybe, her momma would start to smile again.

Seven

Chloe settled into the wide leather seat in the private jet and stretched out her legs.

"Comfortable?" Miles asked as he secured his seat belt.

"You know this is going to spoil me for regular travel anywhere, don't you?" she said archly.

"All part of my nefarious plan," he answered, wiggling his eyebrows like an old-time villain in a black-and-white movie reel.

She laughed. "Well, I have to say that so far I like the sound of your nefarious plan."

He took her hand and squeezed it gently. "Good." Then he sighed, and his expression became more serious. "I'm glad you're with me. I haven't been home since my father's funeral two years ago."

"Do you miss him?"

"He certainly was a force in my life. We didn't always see eye to eye, but he was my father."

Which told her everything and nothing all at the same time and gave her the perfect opportunity to do a little digging.

"Tell me about your family. You are so lucky to have brothers and sisters. And your mother, too, she's still alive?"

"Yeah, my mom's still alive and kicking. She was devoted to my father and nursed him for as long as she was able." A shadow crossed his face. "She took Dad's death hard. They'd been together since my dad was about twenty-two and it was her that helped him focus his energy on starting up Wingate Refineries. After Dad passed away, Uncle Keith, who is a family friend, took her on a tour of Europe, but now she's involved in the family business again.

"Not so sure Uncle Keith is thrilled with that. From what I hear from my siblings, he seems to expect more than friendship from Mom and wants more of her attention. He and Dad were rivals for Mom's affections back in the day. Dad won and he and Uncle Keith remained friends. Since Dad's death he's been a constant support to her but now she's back on her feet, she doesn't need him as much, I guess."

"She sounds formidable."

Miles chuckled. "Not sure she'd like that description, to be honest."

"Well, I'm intimidated already," Chloe said with a smile to soften her words.

She fought back a yawn.

"Hey, the flight is going to be about two and a half hours, once we reach cruising altitude. Why don't you put your seat back and have a bit of a sleep?" Miles suggested.

Chloe felt a blush of heat bloom through her body at the memory of exactly why she was so tired.

"Sounds like a plan. In fact, I may not even reach cruising altitude before I nod off. Must be something to do with the engine noise singing me to sleep."

Miles's lips curved into a smile. "Or something to do with last night."

"A lot to do with last night, I suspect," Chloe admitted aloud. "And if I'm to look anything near respectable when I meet your family, I'll definitely need that nap."

"I'll leave you to it," Miles said, dropping a kiss on her lips as he unclipped his seat belt when the pilot notified them that it was now safe to move around the aircraft. "I'm going forward to have a word with Sam, the pilot."

"Friend of yours?"

"We went to high school together."

"Well, don't distract him from flying the plane, okay?"

Miles laughed. "Duly noted."

When he came back to sit by Chloe, she was fast asleep. He'd noticed the shadows under her eyes this morning, but the sparkle in her eyes had offset that. He couldn't believe how much he enjoyed being with this woman, or how quickly they'd fallen into sync with one another. It had surprised him on so many levels. His business was security. He was a naturally cautious person. And yet, with Chloe, he hadn't felt his usual need to hold back or to run a standard background check like he usually did whenever he considered letting someone into his life.

He settled back in the seat and fastened his seat belt before leaning his chair back and closing his eyes. Being here, next to Chloe, felt right in a world that he knew—for his family, at least—was fast descending into chaos. He'd need his wits about him, going home. But he also knew he needed the quiet strength of the woman beside him to get through it.

When the plane landed in Royal, Texas and taxied to the administration building of the Wingate family's private airport, Miles could see his twin brothers standing on the tarmac, waiting for him. He felt that familiar tug of belonging to something far greater than just himself. The Wingates were a force to be reckoned with, not just in Texas but worldwide, too. But, to Miles, they were his family, and family trumped all things no matter how much he'd tried to distance himself from it.

To be a Wingate meant meeting very high expectations, and he knew his brothers were heartsick about the incident at the plane factory. He only hoped that he could do something effective when it came to studying the necessary data to find out where the security breach had come from.

Miles leaned over and woke Chloe with a kiss on her cheek.

"We're here."

"Oh, already? I feel like I only just closed my eyes. Heavens, I must look a sight. Do I need to freshen up before we get off the plane?"

He let his eyes drift over her face and he shook his head. "No, you look beautiful."

A hint of color tinged her cheeks. "Thank you. You're good for a girl's ego."

"I don't believe in lying and deception. I wouldn't tell you that you were beautiful if I didn't believe it."

Her gaze skittered away from his, as if his words had made her uncomfortable, and she caught her lower lip between her teeth. The action sent a bolt of lust straight to his groin as he remembered biting that same lip only hours ago and remembered, even more vividly, exactly how she'd tasted.

Chloe reached for her tote and gave him an apologetic grin.

"I'm going to need a minute to two, at least."

"If you don't mind, I'll head on out to my brothers." He gestured out the window. "They're obviously eager to see me."

"Oh, of course. And I really will only be a couple of minutes, I promise."

He kissed her again and watched as she got out of her seat and went to the compact bathroom near the rear of the plane. Then, he squared his shoulders and headed out the door.

Sutton, the younger of the twins by only a few

minutes, came forward and clasped his hand before dragging him into a tightly held man-hug.

"Miles, good to see you. Thanks for coming. We've missed you." Then he released his younger brother and stepped back.

"Yeah, I missed you guys, too."

"But not enough to come home more frequently," Sebastian said, coming forward and hugging Miles, also.

"What can I say? All work and no play makes me a very dull boy," Miles countered.

He'd had to face his own demons about his lack of contact with the family since their father's death, but he wasn't about to hash all that out right now.

Sutton issued a low whistle. "Miles, it looks as though you've made some time for play if the lovely lady coming off the plane is any indication. You didn't mention you were bringing company."

Miles turned around and watched Chloe as she donned an oversize pair of sunglasses and slowly walked across the tarmac toward them.

"To be honest, you didn't really give me time to tell you anything. We can stay at the Bellamy if it's going to be a problem."

"Hell, no." Sebastian said quickly. "Mom would never forgive us if we drove you away before you even got to say hi. Besides, she'll be intrigued you brought a girl home to meet her. It's a first for you, isn't it?"

"Yeah," Sutton chimed in. "And since Beth and

Cam have hooked up, Mom's got ideas about all of us settling down."

Miles laughed and turned away from his brothers so he could slide an arm around Chloe's waist and draw her to his side.

"Chloe, I'd like you to meet my brothers. Don't feel bad if you can't tell them apart. Each one is likely to be masquerading as the other at some stage of our stay anyway."

"Now, now, Miles. Don't go giving your guest the wrong impression," Sebastian said as he stepped forward and offered Chloe his hand. "I'm Sebastian. The good-looking one."

Chloe laughed, obviously charmed by his brother's foolishness. "And you must be Sutton?" she said as she shook hands with the other twin.

"Obviously Miles has been talking about us," Sutton drawled as he delivered a killer smile to Chloe. "Don't believe everything he tells you."

Miles felt a prickle of unease tug at the back of his mind. He didn't recall ever telling Chloe his brothers' names, and that was the kind of detail he didn't normally forget. But then again, nothing about his life had been normal since he'd literally bumped into her on Wednesday morning. Besides, it wasn't as if his family wasn't in the news from time to time. He decided to ignore the niggle of doubt and, once their luggage was removed from the plane, they all walked together to the large SUV waiting outside the airstrip to take them home.

Home.

It was quite a concept to most people but for Miles it left his shoulders tense and his mind full of memories of disappointing his father and hearing in no uncertain terms that unless he toed the family line he'd be written off as a failure. What Trent had never understood was that Miles was possibly more like him than any of his other children—strong-minded and determined to succeed on his own merits. Where they differed was that Miles was not prepared to succeed at any cost—even at the expense of others— and that, unfortunately, had been what had driven the permanent wedge between the two of them.

And, despite the warm welcome he'd received, Miles still sensed the invisible gulf between himself and his brothers. They, too, had been unhappy when he'd struck out on his own after finishing college. Not to say that the twins had agreed with their father 100 percent, either, but their methods had been to effect change from the inside. This being made easier, of course, after their father's first stroke, which had given them more of the necessary control to keep Wingate Enterprises at the top of its game. But now the company's position on the ladder was under grave threat.

Miles and Chloe settled into the back of the SUV, and Sebastian and Sutton took the front. As they headed toward home and passed through Royal, Miles noted the familiar landmarks and wished he'd thought to book a room at the Bellamy just so he and Chloe would have some space away from the rest of his family. Yes, the Wingate mansion was huge and the land sprawled over many acres, but he knew he'd be on tenterhooks until they were on a plane back to Chicago again.

He reached across the leather seats and took Chloe's right hand. Even she seemed tenser than he'd known her so far. Her gaze was fixed on the passing scenery and her entirely kissable lips had firmed into a straight line. He leaned over to whisper in her ear. "If you're not comfortable at the house, we can check in at a hotel. Okay?"

She turned her face to his and gave him a brittle smile. "I'll be fine. Just don't abandon me."

"I'll try not to but I will have to go into work with my brothers," he said, keeping his voice low. "If I have to leave you, I'll make sure you're in good hands, I promise. My sister Beth will welcome your company, I'm sure."

"And you have another sister, too, don't you?"

"Yes, Harley. She's living in Thailand at the moment. Both my sisters are heavily involved in charity work."

Sutton looked over from the front passenger seat. "Sharing family secrets, Miles? Or uttering sweet nothings?"

"I apologize. My brother thinks he's a comedian," Miles said as he straightened. He made a point of not letting Chloe's hand go.

Her smile became even more strained, and she turned her attention back out the window. He'd handled this all wrong, and she was clearly overwhelmed by his family's obvious wealth. He knew it made some people uncomfortable. They should have taken a regular flight out of Chicago and hired a car. That way they would have had total independence. Hell, he probably shouldn't have brought Chloe along at all. Talk about baptism by fire. Well, he'd do the job he came to do and that would be it. They'd be back in Chicago and back to discovering all there was to know about each other in no time.

Chloe felt her entire body cringe as they drove onto the Wingate estate. She'd been here once, as a child, the summer before she turned eight and her world, as she knew it, had disintegrated. Trent and Ava Wingate had hosted a massive picnic and invited all their local staff and business associates. There'd been bouncy castles and pony rides and a magician. It had been like a fantasyland and left her completely overwhelmed by everything, and she had clung to her mother like a limpet.

"Don't worry," she heard Miles say from beside her. "It's not as imposing as it looks and I have it on good authority that my family won't bite."

She dragged her thoughts from the past. "Good to know. And, as to imposing? I'll get back to you on that."

The road to the house began to rise slightly, and there on the highest point of the gently rolling hills, stood a large mansion. Oh, it was imposing all right. A mix of Southwestern and California ranch architectural styles, the cream stone and stucco building dominated the knoll on which it was built. It certainly wasn't your average family home.

Sebastian rolled the SUV to a halt outside the front of the building, and Chloe was quick to alight from the vehicle. She drew in a deep breath and was assailed with the scents of home. Pasture, animals, clean air. It was what she'd taken so much for granted growing up. Her family's home hadn't been terribly far from here, and while they hadn't lived anywhere near the grandiose scale of the Wingates, they'd been affluent enough. Until Trent Wingate had done the dirty on her father, she reminded herself and steeled herself for the welcome that was apparent on the face of the woman coming through the front door.

A few inches taller than Chloe, Beth Wingate had a thin but elegant build. Her dark blond hair hung long and straight and she looked amazing in the designer sundress she'd teamed with a matching pair of flat shoes that took a little of the edge off her sophistication.

"Miles! So good to see you!" She flew toward her younger brother and wrapped her arms around him in a hug. "It's been too long since you've been home."

"So y'all keep telling me," Miles answered, hugging her back with a wide grin on his face.

He seemed far more comfortable with his sister than he'd been with the twins, Chloe realized.

Another woman appeared in the doorway. Thin and looking a bit frail, Chloe recognized Ava Wingate immediately. Grief and time had tinged her hair, once the same color as Beth's and Miles's, with gray but her gray-green eyes were sharp and clear. Chloe felt a moment of anxiety. Would Ava recognize her? She'd changed a lot from the shy seven-year-old who'd been here last time. Maybe she should have stopped and thought about this a bit more before suggesting she accompany Miles. She could bump into anyone who'd once known her parents , and she looked enough like her mom that someone might actually recognize her. A sick feeling took up residence in her stomach.

"Miles, welcome home," his mother said as she moved elegantly toward her youngest son. "It's good to have you back. And you've brought company? What a surprise. Welcome, I'm Ava Wingate."

Ava extended a slender hand to Chloe, who took it automatically. The woman might look frail but that handshake was pure steel. Much, Chloe suspected, like the woman herself. She still remembered running away, frightened, from the magician show and straight into the skirts of Ava Wingate. The woman had placed firm hands on Chloe's shoulders and turned her around to face the magician before bending down to whisper in her ear, "Never show fear. Always face it down." Then she'd given Chloe a gentle push back toward the rest of the children.

The advice had stood her in good stead throughout her life even if it wasn't always comfortable. This was definitely one of those occasions.

"Hi, I'm Chloe. I'm sorry if my presence is an intrusion," she said apologetically.

"Well, I can't deny it would be nicer to have met

you under better circumstances. However, you're here now. Please come inside. We can have iced tea and a snack on the patio by the pool while Miles and his siblings discuss what they need to."

Chloe went with her hostess, feeling somewhat like a calf that had been cut from the herd. She cast a glance back over her shoulder to Miles, who was handing their luggage to a staff member who had appeared. He caught her glance and gave her a re-assuring wave. Chloe reminded herself that he had said no one at the house would actually bite, but she was going to have to stay on her toes nevertheless.

On the patio, Ava gestured for Chloe to take a seat in a delightfully shaded area. Shortly after, a woman brought out a tray with iced tea and warm, fresh cookies. Chloe's stomach gave an unseemly rumble and she apologized immediately. Miles's mom merely waved a hand in the air, dismissing the apology before Chloe had finished.

"Please, help yourself. These are fresh from the oven and they're always delicious. Dinner won't be for a couple more hours. Plus, if I know my son, he probably forgot that you need to eat at regular intervals to keep your stamina up. He's a lot like his father was. Driven and focused to the expense of those around them at times. Tell me, have you known each other long? And, how did you two meet?"

Ava's gaze locked onto Chloe like a laser, and Chloe sat a little straighter on the outdoor chair and fought the urge to nervously smooth her hair. She took a sip of her tea and was relieved to see her hand didn't shake.

"Oh, that's lovely," she commented, and gathered her thoughts together. She may as well stick as close to the truth as possible. Less chance of getting caught out. "To be entirely honest with you, Miles and I haven't known each other long. In fact, we only met on Wednesday."

She was pleased to see a flare of surprise in the older woman's eyes. "Tell me more," Ava coaxed. "It isn't like Miles to be spontaneous."

Chloe forced a laugh. "Well, the last few days have certainly been that. We met in the park. He, quite literally, swept me off my feet."

She went into a little more detail about her fall, how solicitous he'd been and how he'd looked after her afterward.

"Good to know he hasn't forgotten everything his family taught him," his mom said wryly. "So you've actually only known one another two days?"

Chloe felt a heated blush stain her cheeks. It might only seem like a couple of days, but they'd been a very intense forty-eight-plus hours. She nodded and took another sip of her tea.

"Well, you certainly must have made an impression."

"She did," Miles murmured as he walked up toward them. He bent to kiss his mother on the cheek. "And we had plans for this weekend."

"Plans that we disrupted. I'm sorry about that, Miles, but we do need your expertise. There's no one else I trust more than you right now," the older woman said solemnly. "After what's happened, we're not sure who is telling the truth anymore."

"I'll do what I can, Mom. I'll go into the office with Sebastian and Sutton tomorrow. We'll need to work fast if the DEA is involved. They may shut everything down before we can—"

Chloe's ears pricked up. The DEA? So it wasn't just a safety issue anymore?

"Let's not discuss the finer points right now," Ava said, cutting Miles off quickly.

Chloe had no doubt it was because she was here.

His mother continued. "I've put you in your old room, Miles. Since you didn't see fit to tell us you were bringing a guest, I wasn't sure where I should accommodate, Chloe."

"She's with me," he said firmly.

Ava looked from her son to Chloe and back again. One finely plucked brow arched in acknowledgment. The older woman rose from her chair. "I'll let the staff know and have an extra setting laid for dinner tonight."

She gave them a regal nod and walked away, her back ramrod straight and disapproval pouring off her in waves.

"I don't think your mother likes me," Chloe said in a small voice.

"Then it's a good thing I do. Chloe, I'm sorry you had to face her so soon after we arrived. I wasn't expecting her to be home, to be honest. She's always at the office until late most days."

"It's okay. I'm not here to please her."

"Does that mean you're here to please me?" Miles's voice dropped an octave, and Chloe felt a shimmer of desire spread through her.

"Well," she replied, "that depends on how close your mom's room is to ours, don't you think?"

Miles laughed out loud. "Don't worry, we're on the second floor. She's on the first."

"Good to know," Chloe said, and grabbed a cookie from the plate on the table. "How about you show me our room. I really will need to freshen up before dinner."

"Sure thing. I could do with a little freshening myself."

Miles offered her his hand and she let him tug her to her feet. He drew her close and bent his head and kissed her deeply. When he pulled away, he said, "I'm glad you're here, Chloe. This would have been tougher without you."

She lifted a hand to his cheek and looked directly in his eyes, for a split second forgetting her real reasons for being here. "I'm glad I can be here for you, too."

He grinned. "Let's go shower."

Eight

Chloe woke alone to tumbled sheets and a sense of satiation she was fast coming to associate with Miles Wingate. Dinner last night had been strained, as if everyone there was on tenterhooks for a variety of reasons to which she was not allowed to be privy. But when she and Miles retired after dinner, all the tension of the evening swiftly dissipated.

She stretched against the sheets before rising from the bed and getting ready to head downstairs. After a quick shower and choosing a cornflower blue sundress she knew flattered her blond hair and blue eyes, she went downstairs.

Beth Wingate was in the breakfast room off the kitchen. She looked up with a friendly smile as Chloe entered the room.

"Good morning. Help yourself to breakfast from the buffet. Mom and the guys have already headed into work."

"Yes, Miles told me last night that they'd be going in early. Do you think he'll be able to help source the problem?"

A small frown pulled between the other woman's brows. "I sure hope so. Say, you'll be at a bit of a loose end today. Would you like to spend the day with me? I can ask Miles to call us when he's heading back to the house."

Chloe pushed down the automatic "no" that sprang to her lips. She wasn't quite sure how to take the friendly overture from Miles's sister, but it was an opportunity to learn more about the Wingate family, which could only help her cause.

"I'd like that, thank you."

"Great! I'm working on a masquerade ball fundraiser for the Texas Cattleman's Club and was planning on heading to the club after breakfast to discuss decorations. I'd appreciate another woman's input."

"I'm not sure how much use I'll be to you," Chloe said on a laugh. "My experience with decorating relates most to second graders in the classroom."

"Well, there's a child in all of us, right?" Beth replied with a warm smile.

"Do you do a lot of fundraising?"

"It's my role in life to part the wealthy from their money for worthy causes. Mom used to manage Wingate Philanthropies, but after my dad had his first stroke, she devoted most of her time to him so it was natural for me to take over. I have to admit I love it. There's a real satisfaction in knowing that what you do makes a difference for those less fortunate. The upcoming ball isn't for a few months yet, but I like to make sure that all my ducks are in a row early on. That way I always have contingencies should anything go awry."

Chloe filled a plate with scrambled eggs and a couple of strips of grilled bacon and sat at the table.

"Contingencies are always a good idea. I'll text Miles and let him know I'm spending the day with you, just in case he comes back here and wonders what I'm up to."

Beth made a face. "Oh, now Mom and the boys have their hooks into him again, I doubt they'll be letting him home early. They really need his expertise. I'm not sure how much Miles has told you, but things are looking pretty dire for WinJet at the moment. Safety is such an important issue."

"And the DEA?" Chloe pressed.

Beth's face froze. "He told you about that?"

"Just a little," she half lied.

"Mom wanted a lid kept on that."

Chloe felt a burst of irritation. "Well, I'm hardly likely to run screaming it from the rooftops," she said stiffly, even as she began to wonder what the reporter who'd written the safety investigation exposé could do with that information.

But did she dare feed that to him? It was exactly the kind of information he was looking for. Chloe's hands bunched into fists on the table. She started as one of Beth's hands settled on hers.

"I'm sorry. I didn't mean to offend. It's just that we're finding it hard to trust anyone right now. What with the safety issues leading to the fire and the hurt caused to our staff and now the DEA being brought in. Someone has betrayed us horribly."

Chloe withdrew her hand from beneath Beth's. "I understand. It's a difficult time for you."

"I'd still enjoy having your company today, if you can forgive me for what I said just now?"

It was clear Beth was trying desperately to make amends. Chloe forced herself to relax and painted a smile on her face.

"Sure, no offense taken."

But she *was* offended. This family took so much for granted and circled the wagons instantly when under threat. But she was on the inside of that circle now. She'd waited all her life for this opportunity, and she was exactly where she needed to be to make a difference to her mom's future. But could she go through with it? Could she deliberately hurt the man who was fast coming to mean a lot more to her than simply a means to an end?

"Well, can you see anything?" Sutton asked as he looked over Miles's shoulder.

Miles pushed back from the computer and huffed out a sigh of irritation.

"I'm not quite sure what you expect of me, Sutton, but trust me, it takes a whole lot more time and focus—*uninterrupted* focus—to look for what I believe you suspect has happened."

"So, nothing?"

Miles closed his eyes and counted to three before opening them again. "I didn't say that. It would seem that someone has tampered with the safety logs at the jet factory."

Sebastian uttered a string of curses while his twin merely paled.

"So it *was* deliberate," Sutton said grimly. "The accident was no accident at all." He swore. "I can't believe someone in our employ would put other people's lives at risk like that. No wonder we're being charged with criminal negligence. This should never have happened."

"What can we do to make sure it doesn't happen again," Sebastian asked.

"Well, we can put some short-term security measures in place, but frankly the entire Wingate IT system needs a major upgrade. Steel Security can do that for you, but it is going to take time and if the DEA—"

"Let's cross that bridge when we get to it. Organize what you can for us for now, and we'll take the next step as it comes." Sebastian rubbed a hand across his face. "Man, this sucks, doesn't it? Tell me, if we'd done the IT upgrade like you'd told us to, could this have happened?"

Miles frowned. "No system is 100 percent hack proof but, to be honest, what you have had running here is child's play."

"So we've been negligent on this as well?" Sutton pressed.

"I wouldn't say negligent. Your staff signs a code of conduct with their contracts, don't they? Whoever did this was in breach of their agreement with WinJet as their employer. If criminal charges need to be laid, it's against whoever did this. And, I suspect, more than one person. The digital footprints are all over the place." Miles rocked back in his chair and looked at his brothers before delivering his final judgment. "To me it looks like a deliberate attack."

"I don't like the sound of that," Sebastian said carefully. "How long do you think this has been going on? After all, we know Dad made some enemies. Is it possible it stems further back, to when he was still alive?"

Miles shook his head. "This looks a lot more recent than that."

Sutton growled. "So this is on us. We've got to find out who is behind this, but before we can do that we have to do right by the men who were injured. Forget the lawyers and trying to beat them down, it's our obligation to settle with the least fuss. We need to take responsibility and then make sure nothing like this can ever happen again."

Sebastian was nodding. "I agree. Mom's in her office. Let's tell her our decision. I know Uncle Keith was advising that we fight the claim and imply it was staff negligence that caused the fire, but the deeper we look into all of this, the less I like it. We tell the lawyers we'll take the hit and admit liability. After all, it happened on our watch."

Miles watched his brothers talk it out and felt a swell of pride grow in his chest. They were nothing like their father. Trent Wingate would have fought paying out until his last breath. He would never have had the grace to admit any level of failure. Maybe Wingate Enterprises stood a chance of being a better, more ethical employer under his twin brothers' guidance than it ever had before.

There was a movement at the door to the office they'd been using, and all three men swiveled round.

"I can't tell you how much it gladdens my heart to see all my boys working together like this," Ava said as she glided gracefully into the office and perched against the edge of Miles's desk.

"Well, don't get too used to it, Mom. I have a business I'm very happy running back in Chicago."

He smiled to take the sting out of his words, but he couldn't help but feel the burr of irritation that she continued, in her not-so-subtle way, to try to lure him back into the family fold. It had been the same way every time he'd come home. As if she and his dad had believed he'd come back eventually and that he just needed to get his misguided burst of independence out of his system. Forget that his company was now worth several hundred million dollars and that he had investors and clientele stretching to every corner of the globe as well as a staff of thousands. Not to mention the fact he'd started his business up, all on his own, without their input or advice or financial backing. One day they'd see him as the success he knew himself to be. At least he hoped so.

Right now, he knew he'd had enough of the cloying atmosphere of the Wingate Enterprises head office. He wanted nothing more than to get back to the house, back to Chloe, and to take her on a long walk or horseback ride far from the house and his family obligations.

"Look, I've done all I can for the time being. I'll get one of my IT security geeks to work on a quick fix for now, and have the team work on something for the entire system in the next couple of weeks."

"And you'll charge us accordingly," Sebastian said with a half smile.

"Of course. No free rides," Miles confirmed, quoting a phrase his father had used far too often while they were growing up.

Sebastian laughed and got up from his chair and clapped Miles on the shoulder. "Come on then, little brother. Let's head home. Mom, are you finished for the day? Can we give you a ride back?"

"No, Keith is coming to meet me. We have some matters to discuss, but we'll see you all at the barbecue tonight."

"You're still going ahead with the annual Fourth of July celebration tonight?" Miles asked.

"We may be in a state of flux, Miles, but we still have a responsibility to observe tradition. We've never canceled before, and we're not about to start now."

There was a vein of strength in Ava's tone that told

him that the world could be ending and she would still keep up appearances. He wasn't sure if he admired her tenacity, or if he thought it more reminiscent of rearranging the deck chairs on the *Titanic*. Either way, he wasn't sure a showy display of wealth from the family was such a great idea right now.

"Well, before we go, let's get you up to speed with what we've decided," Sutton said before briefly outlining everything.

To her credit, Ava listened intently without interrupting. When Sutton was done, she nodded.

"Well, if you think that's best, although it's not what your father would have done," she said softly.

"Mom, we're in charge now. Dad and you have done great work building Wingate Enterprises to where it is today, but Sebastian and I are heading the corporation now. This is our decision and we both stand by it."

Miles could hear the note of frustration in Sutton's tone and wondered just how often their mom had voted the guys down on their decisions so far. She was an astute businesswoman and she'd guided their father for years, when he would allow himself to be guided, that was.

"I understand, Sutton. Look, before you take it to the legal team, how about I run it past Keith? Maybe we can talk about this some more tonight."

A trickle of unease skittered down Miles's spine. "Mom, I know I don't have a pony in this race, but for now I think it's best if we keep this decision between just the four of us until the offer is made to the workers who were hurt."

Ava looked shocked. "Are you suggesting Keith is less than trustworthy? I'll have you remember he is a valued and long-standing member of this company and he's been stalwart at my side since your father died."

"Even so, the evidence is right there. Someone with pretty high clearances tampered with the safety reports. Until we know who it is, nothing we've discussed here today should be shared with anyone. Am I clear?"

Miles held his breath. He'd never used that tone of voice with his mother before, but this was vitally important. No doubt Keith would be furious when he learned that major decisions were being made without his input, but he wasn't the only senior management or adviser being kept out of the loop. Someone had to be responsible for the damage that had been systematically done to Wingate Enterprises. They couldn't be careful enough until they had the information they needed to bring that someone to justice.

"I agree," Sebastian said in support.

Sutton murmured the same.

"Well," Ava said, her eyes bright with indignation. "I suppose I should consider myself fortunate that you've thought to include me in your findings."

"Mom, don't be like that," Miles said.

"Don't be like what? Don't be hurt that a man we've trusted and included as family for longer than each of you has been alive is to be cut out of this?

I don't like it one bit, but I will concede to your directive. For now."

"Thank you," Miles rose from his chair and took his mom's hands in his before leaning forward to kiss her on the cheek. "I'm sorry. I know Keith has been your rock since Dad died, but I know what I'm doing."

He didn't want to add that it was always the people you least expected who could do the most harm.

Nine

Despite their rocky start, Chloe had enjoyed her day with Beth. Miles's older sister was very passionate about what she did, and her enthusiasm pulled Chloe along in her wake as they visited the Texas Cattleman's Club here in Royal and then met with Beth's fiancé, Cam, for lunch at the club. Initially Chloe had felt uncomfortable—as if she was intruding on the newly engaged couple's time together, but Cam had hastened to assure her she was welcome and had shown a great deal of interest in her teaching when he'd heard what she did.

Back at the house, Chloe had decided to make the most of the pristine swimming pool. Her wrist was feeling much better today, and she'd been busy doing laps when she felt a frisson of awareness that told her she was being watched. She glided to the edge of the pool and looked up.

"Oh," she said. "You're back."

A curl of sheer joy unfurled from deep inside as she looked up at Miles. He was dressed for business in a light gray suit and a crisp white shirt that was open at the neck. A pulse of need rippled through her. She couldn't wait to take it off him. But then she noticed the lines of strain on his face and the tiredness in his eyes.

"Nothing wrong with your powers of observation," he teased, and with the light humor she saw some of the tension on his features begin to ease.

"Did you want to swim with me?" she invited.

"Actually, I came to find you to see if you'd like to go for a ride before tonight's barbecue."

"Do we have time? If it's going to be as formal as last night, I'll need plenty of time to get ready. I really wouldn't want to offend your mom."

"It'll be casual and out here on the patio and lawns. We have time."

"Then I'd love to go for a ride with you. I'm assuming you mean on a horse?"

That earned her a belly laugh, and the last of the strain fell away from his face. "Yes, on a horse, although I'm open to suggestions."

"Let's get away from here first and see what comes up."

He didn't miss the double entendre. "I'll make sure I pack a blanket."

He held out a hand to assist her in getting out of

the pool and she dried herself quickly before wrapping the towel around her and hurrying upstairs to get changed. She didn't bother drying her hair, instead twisting it into a loose knot secured with a clip at her nape. Miles wasn't far behind her. He shed his suit and shirt and threw on a pair of jeans and T-shirt together with a pair of boots. Chloe searched her case for her own jeans and a light sweater. She hadn't brought boots so she pulled on a pair of socks and trainers that had seen better days.

"Will these be okay?" she asked, gesturing to her feet.

"Sure, unless you'd like me to see if Beth or Harley has a pair of riding boots lying around that'd fit you. There are always spares at the stables."

"No, it'll just mean it takes longer before we're out on our own. I'll manage," she said, slipping her hand in his. "Let's go."

At the stables she was mounted on a gentle-natured gelding, while Miles, predictably, rode a more spirited animal. Chloe leaned forward and patted her horse's neck. "I hope he's as gentle as you say. It's been years since I've ridden. I'm probably going to be hellishly sore tomorrow."

"We can take it easy," Miles said, urging his mount forward. "I just need to clear my head a little."

"Do you want to ride on ahead at your own pace?" Chloe suggested. "I'm happy to toddle on behind with my new best friend, here."

"No, I want to be with you. You remind me that life shouldn't be all about work."

Chloe fell silent as they walked the horses away from the stables and down the hill toward a small lake on the property. Miles had sounded serious. Very serious. It was a reminder to her that her reasons for being with him were not entirely altruistic, and it left her feeling more confused than ever. When she was with Miles, she wanted to be truly with him, heart and soul. It was easy to forget about the sins of his father and her long held dreams of revenge when they were together.

He only had to be within ten feet of her for her entire body to crave him. And when he spoke she found herself genuinely wanting to listen to what he said. Whether he recited a grocery list or the Declaration of Independence, it would make no difference to her. The timbre of his voice was as alluring to her as his physical attributes. And, of course, those were outstanding. He seemed to know exactly what she needed. She'd never had a lover like him before.

Of course, it wasn't just his physical presence or bedroom prowess that drew her like metal filings to a magnet. He was genuinely good, from what she could tell. In his case, the apple had fallen far, far from the tree. The way he'd treated her from the moment they'd met was a case in point. She had no doubt that he'd feel utterly betrayed if he knew of her ulterior motive in meeting him and inserting herself into his family gathering.

She was beginning to doubt her own motives, too. It was one thing to grow up in a household infused with her mom's desperate unhappiness, which was fueled by anger and a desire to seek recriminations, but quite another to come face-to-face with the perpetrators of those emotions and find they were, in fact, for the most part anyway, decent people. The jury was still out on Ava, Chloe thought to herself. But the woman hadn't been rude or unkind. Instead she'd been deeply protective of her family, not wanting their current dirty laundry to be aired amongst anyone she didn't know she could trust.

Would Chloe have been any different under the same circumstances? She doubted it.

"Are you planning to ride to the border?"

Chloe drew her horse to a halt and looked around, realizing that Miles had dismounted some way back. She laughed and turned her mount and trotted back toward him.

"Sorry, I was away with the fairies."

"Should I be worried you could forget me so easily?"

Miles came over to stand beside her horse and helped her dismount. As she slid from the saddle, her body grazed against his and bursts of heat ignited at each point they touched. She turned and found herself wrapped in his arms.

"No, not worried. I can't remember the last time I felt this relaxed, and that's all because of you. Thank you."

She spoke from the heart and she could see her simple words had struck him, too. He leaned forward and kissed her. At first a simple touch of lips, as if he wanted no more than that for now, but then it was as if he couldn't hold back and his hold on her tightened, crushing her to him as his kiss became more demanding, the pressure of his mouth on hers firmer than before. Chloe welcomed his hot, hungry possession and returned his kiss with equal fervor.

She raised her hands to his shoulders, and beneath her touch she could feel the tension in his body ease and relax a little. Well, most of his body anyway. There was no doubting his arousal, and she felt an answering need beat steadily within her as his tongue dipped and delved into her mouth. Eventually, Miles pulled back and loosened his hold on her.

"I so needed that," he said before letting her go completely.

"Bad day?"

"Helluva day, to be honest."

"Then I'm glad I could help in some way," she murmured.

"Oh, you have no idea how much."

Chloe looked up at him under half-closed lids. "You want to show me?"

"Let me secure the horses and grab the blanket."

He was back at her side in seconds and, taking her hand, he led her to a secluded nook where they would not be immediately visible to anyone. Over his shoulder, Miles had a leather saddlebag, and from it he pulled a blanket and two long-stemmed glasses together with a bottle of champagne.

"We're celebrating?"

"Hell yes, we're celebrating," Miles said with a

smile as he tossed her the blanket to spread out on the ground.

"Care to tell me what, in particular?"

"Is the fact that we've managed to get some quiet time to ourselves not enough for you?"

"Sure, I'll drink to that." Chloe laughed and smoothed the blanket out on their patch of privacy at the edge of the lake.

"And, I'd like to show my appreciation to you, too."

She arched a brow. "Your appreciation? For what?"

"For not running straight back to Chicago when I had to abandon you today." He poured two glasses of the sparkling golden liquid and handed her one. "You're quite a woman and I am very glad I met you."

Chloe's mouth and throat dried, and she found it hard to speak. He was being so lovely. In fact, he was being everything she always told herself she ever wanted in a man. And she was deceiving him. Or was she? She hadn't actually taken any steps to disclose their family secrets, yet. Not that she truly knew anything in any detail, but she had the feeling that it wouldn't take much digging to find the kind of dirt she needed to steer the media in the right direction with respect to the DEA involvement with the family's business. It wouldn't take much to overturn the necessary stones that would do the most harm. And then her mother would be vindicated, wouldn't she?

No.

She couldn't do it.

She couldn't cheat on the trust this man had placed in her. She couldn't destroy the family he loved. She couldn't destroy *him*. And it would surely decimate their growing relationship if she followed through on her plans. She didn't want to do that. She'd felt as if she had been alone for the last twenty years or more. Oh sure, she'd been with her mom, but her mom had depended on her so much and had been so wrapped in grief that Chloe had learned from a young age to shelve her own needs and wants and desires. Now it was her turn. Her time. Hers and Miles's.

She clinked her champagne glass to his and took a long sip, letting the fizz travel over her tongue and down her throat. Imbibing the liquid as though it was her new truth. The seal on her new direction. This thing with Miles, it may not go anywhere, but she owed it to herself to find out, didn't she?

"This is such a beautiful spot," she said, looking out over the water.

"I find it is much improved with the current company."

She smiled coyly. "You really do say the nicest things. It makes me feel special."

"Good," he answered simply.

They sat for a short while, sipping their champagne and watching the birds land on the water, leaving a gentle wake in their stead. With her free hand, Chloe traced small circles on the back of Miles's neck. His skin was warm beneath her touch and she felt connected to him in a way she hadn't experienced with another man before. When their glasses were empty, she took his from him and set them both down in the grass away from their blanket.

"That was delicious, but I find myself craving something else," she said in a low voice as she straddled his legs and gently pushed him back to lie down on the blanket.

"Tell me more."

"Well, technically you were going to show me, remember? But it's a good thing I'm an equal opportunity kind of girl."

A smile spread across his lips and his hands settled at her waist, sliding beneath her sweater to burn like a brand against her bare skin. She sighed a little and leaned down, brushing her lips across his, again and again. Just lightly, teasing. One of his hands slid up her back and cupped the back of her head, drawing her to him and encouraging her to kiss him properly. And, because she wanted to, she did.

She loved kissing him. Loved the taste, the feel, the texture of him. He moved his hand again, clearly enjoying what she offered and happy to take it. She shifted slightly so she could kiss a trail across his cheekbones, then along his jaw and down his throat until she nipped the skin at its base. He groaned in response. Emboldened, Chloe pushed his T-shirt up, exposing his chest. Miles helped her by lifting his torso slightly, and she slid the shirt off him completely and dropped it beside them.

She ran her hands over his shoulders, his arms.

Then skimmed across his belly and back up over his ribs and his chest.

"You are magnificent," she whispered with a reverence that would leave him in no doubt as to just how true the words were that she spoke.

She kissed him again, then. Firmly on the mouth. Taking her time to dip her tongue to duel with his as her hands continued to touch and follow every curve and hollow of his body. Her fingers glided to the waistband of his jeans and his hips bucked beneath her touch.

"Impatient, are we?" she asked, smiling against his lips.

"For you? Always."

She moved her hand over the now-bulging denim of his jeans and gripped him firmly through the fabric.

"We need to do something about this," she whispered, and moved lower on him.

Her fingers dealt with the button at the waistband of his jeans before slowly, carefully, lowering the zipper. Miles lifted his hips as she tugged his jeans down, together with his briefs, exposing his arousal to the warm air and her even more heated gaze. She traced his erection with her fingers, letting her nails graze ever so lightly over his sensitive tip before she lowered to him and took him into the warm, wet cavern of her mouth.

He groaned again and his hips thrust upward, as if he couldn't get quite enough of the sensation of her mouth and tongue on him. Chloe encircled the base of his penis with her hand and slowly let her fingers glide up and swirled her tongue gently over his swollen flesh as she did so. She kept up her momentum, subtly increasing the pressure of her hand and her tongue until she felt him fall apart beneath her.

This was what she wanted for him. Complete abandon. No cares. No stress. No worries. Just the deep satisfaction of knowing someone else could, and would, give him what he most desired. She took her mouth from him and moved to lie with her head on his chest. Instantly his hands were on her and began stroking through her hair, which had begun to slide free from its knot. Then his fingers drifted lower, rubbing circles on her back. She felt him kiss the top of her head.

"I think that from now on this will forever be one of my favorite places in the whole world," he rumbled.

His voice was thick, and beneath her ear she could hear his heart still hammering in his chest.

"Mine, too."

They lay like that for some time—just being in the moment. Listening to the sounds of the birds in the trees and the lazily buzzing insects around them. Reveling in the whisper of the breeze in the trees and shrubs that wrapped them in their own cocoon and the gentle lap of the water on the lake's edge.

And then Miles rolled her onto her side and sat up to kick off his boots and socks and completely remove his jeans.

"I feel overdressed," Chloe said as she stretched out on the blanket.

"You most definitely are. Thankfully, I'm just the man you need to solve that particular issue."

"You are, are you?"

"Indeed. Solving problems, all kinds of problems, is my forte."

"I don't think I've ever met a man with a forte before," she mused.

Miles laughed out loud. "I've never met a woman who could steal the breath clean out of my lungs, send me to heaven and make me laugh all within the space of a few minutes."

"Perhaps that is *my* forte," she teased.

But even though her tone was light, her heart was bursting with the realization that she wanted to be that woman for him. Every day. And, as he began to worship her body, the way she'd worshipped his, Chloe was forced to acknowledge that she was fast losing her heart to Miles Wingate. She could only hope he wanted it as much as she wanted to give it to him.

Ten

They were late back to the house and there was a great flurry of activity around the property as they approached.

"What's happening?"

"That'll be the guys finishing the setup for the fireworks display tonight."

"Fireworks *display*?" she asked. "You mean, like a big display or just the family setting off a few rockets and firecrackers?"

Miles laughed. "A proper display. Family tradition. And heaven knows you can't buck tradition. Mom always invites anyone she knows who isn't attending the Cattleman's Club celebrations to come along. She takes it quite personally if they choose the club over her."

"Um, so how many people are we talking, here?"

"A hundred or so."

"A hundred? That's hardly a casual barbecue," Chloe declared, feeling flustered. "I thought it was only going to be family."

Miles looked at her across the back of his horse as he dragged the saddle off. "I'm sorry. I thought I had told you that the July fourth barbecue and fireworks was an annual thing. Given what's happening with WinJet, I suggested axing it but Mom insisted it was a better idea to keep things running as usual so as to avoid any unnecessary attention."

"Well, I'm certainly going to need more than five minutes to get ready, if I'm going to be suitable for public consumption. I hope I've packed something appropriate."

Chloe lifted a hand and pulled a piece of grass from her hair. Miles put his saddle up on its stand and came over to her, and tugged a couple more pieces from her hair for good measure.

"You look beautiful in anything. Honestly, this is just casual. Just think of it as a family get-together— just with a really big family."

He bent down and gave her a kiss as Ava walked into the stables.

"Well," his mother said with a definite snip in her voice. "So glad you two decided to return on time. The rest of the family is gathering in the living room before our guests arrive. Perhaps you could join them when you're ready."

Without awaiting a response, Ava turned around

and walked back to the house. Chloe chewed her lower lip. Anxiety roped through her stomach, tightening like a boa constrictor. Her eyes met Miles's.

"She really doesn't like me."

"It's not you. She's still mad at me for not joining the family business, and she is mad at whoever has caused the problems at WinJet. Obviously she's really worried, because I've never seen her be so openly rude before. I apologize for her behavior, Chloe. You can be sure I'll call her on it when I get the opportunity."

"Oh, please don't. I don't want to cause any more friction."

"Oh, there's friction aplenty without dragging you into her nest." A muscle ticked in his jaw. "You're a part of my life and I won't have her treat you like that. Not now, not ever."

They finished with the horses and tack and made their way quickly up to the house. After another quick shower, Chloe sorted through the items she'd brought with her and chose a fitted pair of white jeans together with a black sequined tunic and a cute pair of silver ballet shoes. Her hair was a mess so she did what she could to brush it into a bun and used a set of diamanté studded pins to secure it in place. She was quick with her makeup, choosing to accentuate her eyes and not to wear foundation. The blush of warmth from the sun and Miles's lovemaking had given her a glow that made makeup almost redundant. A quick slick of lip color and she was done.

Miles smiled as he waited for her by the bed.

"You're wasted on this crowd, Chloe. Right now, I don't particularly want to share you with anyone."

She smiled back at him, feeling that inner glow expand by several notches.

"You're too good for me," she murmured.

As the words fell from her lips she realized she wasn't being trite. She truly meant it. What would it be like to come clean with Miles—tell him the truth about why she'd inserted herself into his life? He deserved to know, but telling him would mean giving up on all her plans—giving up on finally seeing her mom vindicated and genuinely happy again. Even if she wanted to, Chloe knew she couldn't do that, and it was beginning to tear her apart.

There was a knock at their bedroom door.

"Yeah," Miles called out.

Sebastian's voice floated through the door. "You better hurry on down. Mom's getting antsy."

"Well, we can't have that, can we?" Miles muttered to Chloe with a liberal dose of sarcasm. "We'll be right there," he called back to Sebastian.

"Come on," Chloe cajoled him. "This is obviously important to her. Let's not be any later than we already are."

"I like you more and more every minute, you know that?" Miles said, taking her hand and leading her out of the room. "Mom was outright rude, and you're still prepared to play nice and soothe her sensibilities?"

"Miles, I'm a guest in her house, and I'm here

with her son. I don't want to do anything to upset her."

"And I won't stand for her upsetting you, either. You know that, right?"

"I don't deserve you," she whispered, and squeezed his hand tight.

They were at the bottom of the stairs and people were pouring through the front door and being directed by additional staff out through the back to the patio and pool area where the barbecue had been set up.

"Looks like we're right on time," Miles remarked as they moved through the crowd and headed in the same direction.

Outside, the entire area had been converted with a patriotic and festive scene. Red, white and blue bunting hung from the veranda overhang and the uprights were wound with ribbons.

"Your family really goes all out, huh?" Chloe said, looking around her.

"Yes, we do," Ava answered, drawing up from behind.

Chloe started in surprise. She hadn't even seen the woman coming nearer.

"Mrs. Wingate, the decorations look wonderful."

"Thank you." Ava inclined her head graciously. "I don't think you've met our good family friend, Keith Cooper, yet, have you? Keith, come on over and meet the young lady Miles brought down from Chicago with him."

A tall man, with the remnants of an athletic build,

extracted himself from the people he'd been talking to and walked over to Miles and Chloe.

"Keith, this is Chloe Fitzgerald. Chloe, this is Keith Cooper."

Cooper offered his hand to Chloe and gave her a quick handshake. He only took the tips of her fingers, not even offering her the courtesy of a proper handshake. It was something that always bothered her when she met certain men. As if they thought the little woman couldn't handle a full-on palm-to-palm grasp. Personally, she found it disrespectful.

When Mr. Cooper let her hand go, he snaked a possessive arm around Ava's waist. Chloe felt Miles stiffen beside her at the familiarity.

"Keith is an old family friend. He and Dad went way back. In fact, they were rivals for Mom's hand in marriage," Miles pointed out quite deliberately.

Chloe could feel an undercurrent vibrating in the air between the three others.

"And the better man won the fair maiden," Keith said with a wide smile.

But Chloe could see the smile didn't quite reach his eyes.

"If you'll excuse me, I need to speak to the caterers for a moment," Ava said, smoothly extracting herself from Keith's touch.

The man turned his attention to Chloe.

"Fitzgerald, name sounds familiar. You're from Chicago, you say?"

"Yes, I teach elementary school there."

"Hmm, and we've never met? You kind of look familiar."

Chloe felt her blood turn to ice in her veins. She'd been told often enough that she looked like her mother. Had this man ever met Loretta Fitzgerald? Had he known her dad? If so, he could potentially expose her right now. Here in front of everyone. That wasn't how she wanted to do things. When she told Miles the truth of her identity, she wanted that to be in privacy.

"I'm sorry, I've never had the pleasure," Chloe forced herself to respond as smoothly as she could. "And Fitzgerald is a fairly common name. Those Scots travelled far and wide, didn't they?"

The man laughed. "They certainly did. Still, I'm sure if I know you from somewhere it'll come back to me. It always does."

Someone from over by the oversize barbecue hailed him, and he turned and waved to them before making his excuses and leaving Miles and Chloe to themselves. She watched him walk away, feeling as though a ticking time bomb had been activated inside her. Keith Cooper must have known her parents. If he was as close to the Wingate family and as entrenched in the business as he appeared to be, he probably would have known about Trent Wingate's offer to her father, too. And he'd have known what had happened next when that offer had failed to materialize.

A bitter taste flooded her mouth, and she gladly accepted the glass of champagne Miles took from a passing waiter and offered her. She downed half of it in one desperate gulp.

"Thirsty?" Miles asked with a quizzical look on his face.

"I probably should have started with water," she said, forcing a laugh. "I promise I'll go slower with the rest."

He leaned forward and kissed her cheek. "I don't blame you for reaching for a little liquid courage. My family en masse is quite enough, but with all of the hangers-on as well? It makes a good case for drinking. Come on. Let's go check out the buffet."

Chloe nodded and tucked her free hand in the crook of his arm and fought the sensation that she was rapidly losing control of the world around her. It was clear that she really hadn't thought things through properly. While her mom had severed ties with everyone back here in Royal when they'd moved to Chicago, people could still remember her and a gathering like this was bound to prompt memories. Chloe could only hope that no one connected her to the late John Fitzgerald, and she also wanted to distract Miles from possibly pressing her more about how Cooper might have known her.

"Miles, I got the impression you're not all that happy about Mr. Cooper and your mom?"

He firmed his lips before replying.

"He and Dad were cut from the same cloth. Maybe I just see too much of my father in him. I can't help feeling he's just been biding his time until the coast was clear so he could win Mom back, and I think the way he is around her now, a little too familiar. He—" Miles paused for a moment choosing his words carefully. "He doesn't have the best track record with women. Keith's been married and divorced three times, and he's known to have a temper."

"You know, watching them, I don't think you need to worry. Your mom isn't as into him as he is into her."

"Let's hope you're right."

Miles looked up as Sebastian joined him for breakfast. His brother looked tense. In fact, it had been a tense week all round. Everyone had been walking on eggshells, waiting to see whether the DEA would lay charges against WinJet or not. Tempers had been frayed, and even family dinners in the evenings had failed to create the bonhomie that his mother had so prided herself on.

"Any news?" Miles asked, putting his coffee mug down on the table.

"Yeah, I heard just now. They're preparing the case to officially charge us with drug trafficking."

"What? No. There's been a mistake."

Sebastian looked as if he'd aged ten years overnight. "No mistake. A large supply of drugs was found concealed in cargo holds of three planes nearing completion. They say the street value is estimated at millions of dollars."

Miles let out a long, low whistle. "What happens now?"

"We tell our very expensive team of lawyers to

fight the charges for us and fight hard. Oh, and if the charges aren't bad enough, WinJet's assets are tainted by what the DEA have deemed probable drug trafficking. They're freezing the company's assets with a view to forfeiture if we're found guilty."

"They can't actually seize property until you're found guilty, though, right?"

Sebastian nodded. "But when the asset freeze becomes public knowledge, there won't be enough damage control in the world to save us. WinJet can't continue to trade under the freeze. All the company's real estate and accounts will be inaccessible to us. I'm not going to lie to you. This, and the roll-on effect, is going to hit us hard."

"Have you told Mom and Sutton yet?"

"No, and I'm not looking forward to it. Miles, I really need you to up your game on finding out who is behind the safety report tampering. I can't help feeling the fire and the drugs are somehow tied together."

Miles shook his head. "I'm doing what I can but I have to be careful, too. If the DEA discover me poking around in your systems, especially now, they're going to think I'm trying to hide something. Aside from what that might do to my own company, it wouldn't be a good look for the family if we're not seen to be doing the right thing from the outset."

Sebastian sighed. "You're right. We'll have to issue some kind of preemptive announcement— make it abundantly clear that we're innocent and that we're assisting the DEA in any way we can."

"What's this?" Ava asked as she joined them in the breakfast room. "Of course we're innocent. As to assisting the DEA—"

"Mom, we will be assisting them inasmuch as we're capable. They've decided to file charges." Sebastian quickly filled her in on the details. "To be obstructive would only make everything worse."

"Of course it would," she said, coming to stand by her firstborn and putting a hand on his shoulder. "I—"

His mom halted what she was going to say as Chloe came into the room.

"Good morning, everyone."

Miles watched as Chloe halted in her steps and looked at each of them in turn. It was obvious she could feel the tension in the air.

"I think I might have my breakfast on the patio, today," she announced with a forced smile.

"Thank you, Chloe," Ava said graciously. "The boys and I have some business to discuss."

"Of course," Chloe replied brightly. She made up a bowl of cereal and milk and grabbed an apple from the bowl on the sideboard. "Let me know if you need me," she directed at Miles.

He nodded in response. He wished, more than anything, that he could join her outside in the morning air. Summer mornings like this had always been his favorites when he still lived at home.

"We won't be long," he said firmly, letting his mother and brother know that he wasn't about to be dragged into a day-long discussion about the whys and wherefores of what they were going to do next.

After Chloe had left the room, he faced them both. "Look, there's nothing more I can do from here. I can support you just as well from my office in Chicago. I think Chloe and I should head back. Today, if possible."

"No, please reconsider," Ava pleaded. "Zeke and Reagan's engagement party is tomorrow night. At least stay until then. You know Zeke would appreciate it, and it's vital we continue to show a united front as a family."

And there it was, his mother's not-so-subtle form of pressure when it came to family obligations. With everything that had been happening, Miles had forgotten about his cousin's recent engagement.

"I'll speak with Chloe and let you know what we decide."

"Surely you can answer for the girl."

Miles pinned his mother with a look. "I wouldn't be so presumptuous. She was kind enough to travel here with me, and I will be courteous enough to check with her about our plans for our departure home."

"This is your home."

"It might have been once, Mom, but it isn't anymore. I made another life for myself in Chicago a long while ago. One you're actually welcome to see if you'd come to visit. I have a guest room for you, should you ever decide to do that. We're quite civilized up there, you know—hot and cold running water and all that. We even have theaters."

He smiled to soften his words but he could see his words had struck the right chord. His mom was too used to calling the shots with her kids the way she called the shots in business. There were times in the past when they'd all wanted a bit more motherly compassion from her. Thankfully, they'd had that from their aunt Piper, who was nineteen years Ava's junior. Piper had been raised by Ava after their parents died and was far more maternal than her older sister. But Ava's stubborn belief that the fact Miles had made a new life for himself away from the family was merely a temporary aberration drove him crazy. Would she ever accept he was an adult capable of making his own choices?

"Maybe I'll visit when things settle here a little," Ava hedged.

"And if things don't settle?" Sebastian asked bluntly.

"Let's not borrow trouble. We're a strong family and we have powerful connections. Don't ever discount that. We'll get through this, and we'll be even better than before."

Miles could only hope she was right. Wishing for it was one thing, but with the writing on the wall and no way to conduct their own investigation without drawing unwelcome attention to their activities, he had the feeling she was clutching at straws.

Miles finally extricated himself from the meeting with Ava and his brothers and went outside to find Chloe. He was relieved to see she was still out on the patio by the pool. He plonked himself down on the chair beside her and sighed heavily.

"Everything okay?" she asked, reaching out to put her hand on his arm.

Beneath her touch he felt himself begin to calm. He was learning to appreciate that about her. Her touch could do so many things to him and for him. Incite his senses or soothe them, as she was doing now.

"Yes and no."

"Care to explain?"

"Yes, because I'm with you now. No, because my family is facing a truckload of trouble."

"To do with the fire?"

"Among other things." He shook his head. He didn't want to discuss it but understood that Chloe might be curious, and he didn't want to shut her out completely. "This is going to be made public at some stage, but for now I can't tell you more than this. The WinJet plant won't be operating for a while. The investigation has led to it being frozen until certain factors have either been proven or otherwise."

Chloe looked shocked. "But what about the staff? The customers?"

"Exactly. We have a lot to work out." He realized he'd used the word "we" and immediately amended it. "At least my mom and brothers do. As to the rest of us, we're needed for support. Mom asked if we can stay on to attend my cousin Zeke's engagement party tomorrow night—show a strong family front and all that. I'm happy to do whatever you prefer. We can head home right now, or stay a few extra days."

"Miles, you know I'll do whatever makes you happy."

He smiled at her response. "And you do it very well."

She slapped him lightly on the shoulder. "That wasn't what I meant. Look, if you need to be with your family, then we'll stay. Family is important. Everything, really. Sometimes you do things you'd rather not have to do, just to keep them happy. Which reminds me, I need to report in to my mom."

That was a strange choice of words, Miles thought as Chloe rose and left to make the call. And there'd been an odd undertone to her voice. Maybe it was wistfulness, but his spider senses suggested there was more to it. Miles shook his head slightly to rid himself of the sensation. Clearly, he'd been around his family too long already—he was beginning to see discord in everything and Chloe had nothing to do with it, did she?

Eleven

Chloe made her way slowly upstairs. She wasn't looking forward to making that call. Her mom had been so excited when she'd learned that Chloe was going to Royal with Miles so she could get closer to the Wingates and find the leverage she needed to really do them some harm. By the way things were going, though, they didn't need any help in that regard.

She'd heard far more than she was meant to this morning, thanks to an untied shoelace that she'd attended to before entering the breakfast room. Sebastian's words about the DEA and the company asset freeze had been shocking. Chloe hated seeing the strain on Miles, too. This entire issue had ballooned beyond everyone's imagination.

But were they innocent? It was hard to tell. Surely, with the volume of drugs involved they must have known something. And the DEA—they weren't in the habit of laying charges without a solid basis for doing so. Someone in the family had to know something and that would make them just as heartless as she'd always thought they all were. And, as much as she was drawn to Miles and as much as she didn't want it to be true, maybe he was exceptionally good at lying and projecting a false facade. Heaven only knew his father had been—after all, her father had trusted Trent Wingate implicitly. Maybe the apple hadn't fallen far from the tree at all.

A deep ache started in her chest at the thought. She was on the verge of giving her heart to the man, despite her initial intentions. And he'd confounded her at every turn. He'd been solicitous, kind and the type of lover women usually only read about in novels. She didn't want to believe that he was complicit in this in any way. But, she reminded herself, the second his family had crooked a finger, he'd come running to help.

Of course, that didn't tell her anything other than the fact that he was essentially a good man, one part of her argued. Or maybe it told her that he needed to be here to cover his bases regarding his own involvement in whatever was going on. So, what was she to do? Her mom expected her to take action and Chloe had the contact details of the reporter at the paper. All she had to do was send a text or an email to him about what she'd overheard this morning and the Wingate's privacy would be blown wide-open before they had a chance to do damage control.

She picked her phone up from inside her handbag and stared at the blank screen. All her life she'd been bitter about this family, but flawed as they were, were they any different to her own, or any other family? Sure, they had more money than most—a lot more, and much of it amassed on the misery of others—but did she have the right to stomp all over them and expose this latest scandal to the press?

Chloe jumped and nearly dropped her phone as the screen lit up with her mother's face and her mom's special ringtone split the air.

"Hi, Momma," she said, accepting the call. "I was just going to call you."

"Since you hadn't called me, I thought I'd better phone you and check in."

There was no doubting the unhappiness in her mom's voice.

"I'm sorry," Chloe hastened to say. "It's been… busy here."

"I wish I could say the same. Here it's still the same old, same old. I got my utilities bill today. I don't know how I'm going to settle it or how much longer I'm going to be able to support myself."

The ache that had started in Chloe's chest earlier hardened into a painful knot. She knew her mother's financial position better than anyone.

"We'll find a way, Momma. I promise." She thought about the credit card she kept only for emergencies and which she'd painstakingly just paid off.

"And you know you can live with me if you can't afford your apartment anymore."

Her mom sighed. "I'll manage, just like I always have. Anyway, I don't want to talk about it. How are things in Texas? Has Royal changed much?"

"I guess it must have, Momma, because I haven't seen anyone I recognize yet. But then again, I was so young when we left."

Her mom sighed down the line. "It was wrong what they did to us, Chloe. So wrong. We deserved so much better. Your *father* deserved so much better."

And with those words Chloe knew she had to do something, even if it wasn't directly. She could give her mom the ammunition. Loretta then just needed to aim and send it in the right direction. Her mom had lost everything she'd ever held dear, aside from Chloe. Now she had the power to actually give her something back that might bring joy back into her life even if it destroyed the untried bond that was growing between her and Miles.

"Momma, I'm going to tell you something I learned today. Something about the Wingates."

"You are?"

For the first time in a long time, Loretta Fitzgerald sounded thoroughly animated. Chloe swallowed against the bitter taste in her mouth.

"Yes, I am. But I want you to think carefully about what you want to do with this knowledge. This could change things for the Wingates forever."

"The way they changed everything for us?"

Chloe closed her eyes against the sting of tears that suddenly burned there. "Yes."

She repeated what she'd overheard this morning. At the end of the line, her mother gasped.

"So why aren't you giving that information to the reporter that you told me about?"

"Because it's not my fight anymore, Momma. I'm handing it over to you. I can't do it. I'm too close…" Her voice trailed off as her throat thickened, making it hard to speak.

Understanding began to filter through her distress. She'd said it wasn't her fight anymore, but maybe it never had been. And it certainly didn't need to be now. Especially not when she realized her feelings for Miles were genuine. She'd passed the baton to her mom, what Loretta did with it was entirely up to her. For herself, Chloe would explain everything to Miles when they got back home to Chicago and then she'd accept the consequences of her actions. She could only hope that he could see what had driven her to do this—and forgive her all the same.

"Chloe, I warned you about getting hurt. Those people are ruthless."

"No, Momma. They're just people. Yes, Trent Wingate let Daddy down when he most needed support. But he's gone now."

"You're falling in love with that Miles Wingate, aren't you?" There was a definite accusatory tone in her mother's voice. "What about me? What about what they owe me?"

"I've given you the information you need to take

your revenge, if you're prepared to go through with it. But I'm not doing it, Momma. I can't. It's just not right." Tears were flowing down Chloe's cheeks now. She couldn't take anymore. "I'm hanging up now. I'll be home by the end of next week. I hope that's okay."

"It'll have to be, won't it," her mother answered snippily.

"Don't be angry with me, please."

"I'm not angry—just disappointed. We've talked about this for so long. You've been just as determined as I was to take revenge if the opportunity came along."

"I know, and that's my cross to bear. Look, I have to go. I'll talk when I can."

She ended the call and threw her phone on the bed before going through to the adjoining bathroom and washing her face. Man, she looked a wreck. Every one of the emotions tumbling through her—sorrow, regret, guilt—was evident in the blue eyes staring back at her. Chloe started as Miles's reflection appeared next to hers.

"What's wrong?"

Chloe scrambled for a valid reason to be standing in the bathroom, crying. "Mom had some bad news."

"Oh no. I'm so sorry. Do you need to go her? I can arrange it for you."

He was already sliding his phone out of his pocket, but she turned and put a hand on his to stop him.

"No, it can wait until we're back."

"Are you sure? I can book a ticket back to Chicago for you right now. You only have to say the word."

"Please, don't. I'm staying with you, okay? Besides, there's nothing she can do right now."

Nothing except destroy the growing hope Chloe had for a future with Miles.

Miles watched from near the bar as Chloe chatted with Beth and Cam. He could barely take his eyes off her. She was wearing the same beaded black dress she'd worn to the blues evening, and it brought back some darn potent memories right now. He wondered just how long they'd have to stay here before they could slip away and create some new ones. There was a faint smile pulling at his lips as he contemplated just what those memories would entail.

"Penny for them?"

Miles straightened and held his hand out to his cousin Zeke. The son of Ava's late brother, Robert, and his also deceased African American wife, Nina, Zeke and his brother, Luke, were both tall, handsome men who embraced their biracial heritage with pride and confidence. Zeke was the Vice President of Marketing at Wingate Enterprises, and he'd been none too pleased about the revelations in the family meeting Sebastian called late yesterday afternoon. He had his work cut out for him trying to find a way to put a positive spin on the company going forward.

Despite the fact this was a family celebration and the guests were supposed to be family friends, there'd been murmurs and finger-pointing about what had happened with the fire at the jet plant already and he could feel the divide beginning to grow.

It wouldn't be long before the asset freeze was being bandied about, too.

"I was contemplating the job you have ahead of you, spin-doctoring Winjet out of this mess," Miles said with genuine sympathy.

"We have our work cut out for us," Zeke said with a heartfelt sigh. "But we'll get through it. Maybe not exactly unscathed, but hopefully close to it."

Despite the positivity in his cousin's words, Miles couldn't help but feel things were beginning to teeter on the edge of a dangerous precipice. But then he gave himself a mental shake. They were here to keep up appearances and to celebrate Zeke's engagement to Reagan. He needed to chill out a bit. His eyes tracked across the room, back to Chloe.

Zeke turned to follow Miles's gaze.

"She's pretty. Luke and I were surprised you risked bringing her home to meet us."

"Risked?" Miles asked with a raised brow.

"Well, you know what Aunt Ava's like. Has she checked Chloe's pedigree and breeding options yet?"

Miles laughed out loud, earning inquisitive looks from many of the people milling around them. "No, but there's still time. We're staying on an extra few days."

"Well, good luck, cuz. If she's worth it, look after her."

"Oh, I plan to, for as long as she'll let me."

Across the room, Chloe had begun to work her way over toward him and Zeke. A few people smiled or nodded to her, but there were equally as many who turned their backs. Watching it made Miles's hackles rise. Chloe was his guest. Under normal circumstances, that meant she should be welcomed with open arms, but with everything that was going on, she was being treated by some as a rank outsider.

She had a smile painted on her face as she drew closer to them, but he could see that it wasn't reflected in her eyes. In fact, her gaze showed just how angry she was.

"I can't believe the nerve of some people," she fumed.

"Oh?"

"Outside of your immediate family everyone here is a stranger to me, and yet several people tonight have warned me not to trust y'all and to run for the hills. And they're not kidding, either. If it had been said in jest I wouldn't have minded, but these people, these *leeches*, are standing here eating and drinking what your family has provided and they still have the audacity to speak to me like that?"

All of a sudden, she realized that Miles wasn't alone.

"Oh heavens, look I'm sorry. That was very rude of me, and here I am complaining about your guests. Hi, I'm Chloe, and you're Zeke, right? Congratulations on your engagement."

"Don't apologize to me," Zeke said smoothly. "I'm just as annoyed as you are. But I guess this is high society, right? The loyal and the not-so-loyal rubbing shoulders and all playing as if they're friends in the same sandpit."

"Well, I wouldn't mind kicking a bit of sand in a few eyes tonight," Chloe growled. "But, enough of that. How exciting to be engaged and how lovely to have something cheerful, like a wedding, to look forward to in amongst all the turmoil. Have you two set a date?"

Miles felt Zeke shift a little, betraying his discomfort with the question. Was Zeke having second thoughts? Last month, Zeke had shared the surprising news with his cousins that his and Reagan's engagement and their forthcoming marriage were purely born of convenience to help Reagan access her grandmother's inheritance. But Chloe wasn't to know that and it wasn't Miles's secret to share.

"Reagan's mother has stipulated a six-month engagement so it gives her sufficient time to organize the wedding on their property. We're happy to go along with that although we had hoped to marry sooner."

After a little more small talk, Zeke excused himself to go mingle further with the crowd, and Chloe sneaked in close by Miles's side. Slipping an arm around her waist, he smiled down at her as she took a small sip of the champagne she held in her hand. But there was a brittle air to her, which he'd noticed since yesterday after she'd talked to her mother. Obviously, something was worrying her, and equally obviously she wasn't prepared to share that with him just yet.

It frustrated him. He wanted there to be no secrets between them, but he could hardly complain when he hadn't been fully forthcoming about what his family were dealing with. Chloe had been a breath of fresh air in his life right from the beginning, and he was starting to think that he'd like to keep her there, maybe even forever. He turned the idea around in his head. Yeah, *forever* had a nice ring to it. Clearly, they still had so much to learn about one another, but if the way he felt about her and the way he believed she felt about him were any indicator, it wasn't impossible to think that they could have a future together.

He splayed his fingers across her hip and pulled her in even closer.

"You okay?" she asked. "I hope no one's been rude to you, too."

"Not to my face but I've heard a few things here and there. I guess all of us have. In a place as close-knit as Royal it's only to be expected. Some have been jealous of the Wingate family's success and sought to pull us down a peg or two, and something like this is bound to bring out both the best and the worst in people."

She stiffened at his words. "Jealousy?"

"Sure, a lot of people say my dad built his success on the misery of other people's failures. I'll admit, he wasn't perfect all the time, but he was a darn hard worker, and so is Mom. In fact, the entire family has a strong work ethic no matter what they're doing."

"No matter what?"

"Obviously I don't mean at the expense of anybody else, but business is business. Sometimes you have to be ruthless to get ahead. Anyway, we're not here to talk business. We're supposed to be celebrating my cousin and his fiancée's happy future."

A small frown furrowed her brow. "Miles, do you think you'll all have a happy future? I mean, with everything that's going on and all? I don't know exactly what's going on, of course, but it doesn't take a genius to figure out that something is really upsetting your family."

"We'll get through it," Miles said firmly. "We Wingates always do."

Twelve

Later that night, after they'd made love and Miles had drifted off to sleep still holding Chloe in his arms, she played his words over and over again. Yes, there was that air of entitlement she'd always expected from the Wingate family. But it hadn't rankled with her as much as she'd anticipated. She'd seen for herself this past week how hard everyone worked and how strongly they pulled together when the chips were down.

Being an only child, she'd had to be the sole emotional support for her mom. Yes, her mom had the distant family members who'd provided a roof over their head after they'd relocated to Chicago, and provided the hand-me-down clothing that had been Chloe's and her mom's sole source of wardrobe for the first five years after the move. But there'd always been a sense of being beholden to them—that they were a charity case, not family. There hadn't been the extensive network of siblings or cousins to share her troubles with.

Watching Miles and his family pull together toward a common goal, even though there was clearly some tension between them, was something she kind of envied. Although she certainly didn't envy them the storm of negative interest that was about to deluge them soon.

She wondered if her mom had followed through on sending what Chloe had told her to the reporter. She truly hoped not. Of course, she might just be indulging in false hope. Loretta had sounded pretty darn mad on the phone. She wanted her pound of flesh. Even if she never saw any financial compensation, she wanted the Wingate's name to be dragged through the mud and back again. She wanted them to know shame. After all, hadn't that been what had happened with Chloe's family?

She sighed and turned away from Miles, suddenly unable to bear the turmoil of the double life she'd been living since she'd met him. This wasn't her. Not deep down. Yes, she'd had her plan for revenge, but that was before she began to know the family and understand them a little better. She now knew with certainty that she was falling in love with Miles. Deeply and truly.

He was everything she'd ever dreamed of in a man. But she honestly couldn't hope for a future with him until everything was open and honest between them. She'd told herself she'd tell him the truth when they got back home—she had to wait until then. He was dealing with so much right now with his family. Laying out her own motivation for meeting him now would be another burden for him to bear and she simply couldn't do that to him. Not yet, anyway. Eventually, listening to Miles's steady breathing, she drifted off to sleep.

The next few days were quiet around the house. Everyone appeared to be waiting for the next ax to fall. She and Miles made the most of the quiet, heading out riding each morning and spending part of each afternoon lazing around the pool.

Chloe was relieved, the following Wednesday, when Beth invited her to lunch with Gracie, her personal assistant. Beth and Chloe drove to the Texas Cattleman's Club and met Gracie in the foyer outside the restaurant. Beth and her assistant were obviously close, and the warmth in their greeting to one another was a balm to Chloe's soul. No fear of veiled insults or snide remarks to be expected here, she realized. She felt herself physically relax as the tension in her body dissipated.

Gracie was gorgeous, but seemed to be totally unaware of the looks her glossy, long, brown hair and perfectly balanced features drew from passersby. And the way she held her slightly taller than average frame was incredibly elegant. Gracie was effusive in her greeting to Chloe, putting her instantly at ease and treating her as if she'd always been a part of Beth's extended family.

After they were shown to their table, Gracie and Beth briefly discussed Beth's plans for the upcoming masquerade ball.

"I know it's months away, yet," Beth said. "But, with all the rumors flying around, I'm worried about the impact my family's involvement may have on the success of the outcome."

"Beth, don't worry," Gracie said, putting her hand on top of her friend's. Chloe could see the genuine concern in her eyes. "People won't boycott the ball. It's for a great cause."

"But we're associated with the money trail and with the way things are going—"

"No. Stop that. The gala is going to be a great success. We'll make sure of it. Okay?"

Chloe looked up as a tall and very handsome man walked over to their table. He had jet-black hair, closely cropped to his well-shaped head, and his muscular build sat comfortably beneath a distinguished suit that hugged his shoulders like a lover's caress. Beth saw Chloe staring and followed her gaze.

"Ah, Grant," she acknowledged as he drew closer to the table. "It's good to see you. Chloe, I don't believe you've met Doctor Grant Everett, yet? Grant, this is Chloe Fitzgerald. She's visiting with Miles at present."

"Ladies," he said with a nod. "Look, I don't want to take up your time but, Beth, I just wanted to say that your family has my full support, and I know there are many other club members who feel the same way. You guys do great work and you're well respected for what you give back to the community."

Chloe saw tears spring to Beth's eyes.

"Thank you, Grant. That means a lot to me."

He nodded again. "Please pass on my regards to the rest of your family."

"I will."

The three women watched as the doctor moved away from the table.

"It's a sin," Gracie said solemnly.

"A sin?" Chloe asked, confused.

"That a man should be that good-looking and single."

The three women laughed at Gracie's comment, but then Gracie got serious.

"Beth, see? That's what I mean. You have the support of so many people. You seriously don't need to worry about the fundraiser. And if every person in support of your family makes it clear they won't listen to the lies or speculation, it'll soon die down."

Beth gave her assistant a weak smile. "Well, I certainly hope so. Cam has thrown his full support behind us, too but I still worry that we won't be welcome in Royal society for much longer."

"Anyone who turns their back on you, turns their back on me, too. We don't need them in our lives."

"Bless you, Gracie. You're my rock."

"And speaking of rocks. How's Sebastian coping?"

Chloe noticed there was more than a little interest in the tone of Gracie's question. Maybe there was some exasperation there, too? She wondered what that was about.

"You see him as a rock?" Beth said with a giggle.

"Yup," Gracie said lightly. "He's strong, reliable and generally immovable once he's on a course of action. This business will be tearing him up inside."

"He's doing everything he can to get to the root of who's responsible. Together with Sutton and Miles, they're constantly having meetings. Not having access to the WinJet offices and computers anymore is frustrating them intensely."

Chloe flitted a glance to Beth and then across to Gracie. Did Gracie know the full extent of what was happening? Chloe had the impression from Ava and from Miles's reticence to discuss the matter with her in much detail, that the family had closed ranks on talking about what was going on with outsiders. But then again, as Beth's assistant, maybe Gracie wasn't considered to be an outsider. Not like Chloe was.

Beth must have noticed the concern on her face because she said, "It's okay. Gracie is up to speed on everything. I trust her with my life."

"And Mrs. Wingate, how's she managing?" Gracie asked with obvious concern.

"Well, you know my mom. Always presents like a swan gliding along the surface without a care in the world, while all the time she's pedaling flat out beneath the surface of the water. I have noticed, though, she's leaning more and more on Uncle Keith. I can't say I'm happy about it. Aunt Piper assures me that Mom just sees him as a friend. I can only hope she's right, because as a partner, Uncle Keith is all wrong for her."

Beth shook her head. "Look, we didn't come here to talk about Wingate business. We came here to celebrate you. So let's celebrate."

"Good, I'm in a mood to celebrate. Shall we have champagne with our lunch?" Gracie suggested.

"Champagne for lunch. I'm in! What are we celebrating?" Chloe asked.

"Gracie recently had a healthy win in the lottery," Beth disclosed quietly. "She's just received her check and I'm expecting her resignation any day now."

"*Healthy* win? It was an obscene amount of money," Gracie confirmed with a broad grin. "And as to my resignation, I haven't decided what to do yet, so you're stuck with me for a while longer."

"Wow, congratulations, Gracie! How does it feel to be a winner? I don't know if I could even comprehend how to manage something like that, although I'd probably start with sending my mom on a fabulous vacation," Chloe said with a happy smile.

Gracie grinned back. "Well, I'm doing something like that. I'm sending my mom and baby brother to Florida to live near my aunt. I'm buying them a beautiful house and sending my brother to an exclusive private boys' school, where he'll get the opportunity to really make something of himself."

Chloe could feel the enthusiasm and joy pouring off the other woman as she shared her plans. "That sounds fantastic. They must be so excited. And will you go down there, too?"

"Right now I'm undecided. What with the ball and everything, I don't feel like it's a good time to abandon Beth."

"For which I'm grateful, Gracie, but you can't put your life on hold for me. You need to follow your own heart. Find a man to love and want to settle down with. Have a family."

Gracie's eyes grew misty, and Chloe couldn't help but feel that she was very probably thinking of one particular person. Was it Sebastian?

"You know I've always wanted kids, but with all the guys suddenly turning up in my life since the lotto win, I'm not sure if I could trust anyone not to be with me just for my money. Sometimes I think it might just be easier to make an appointment with our friend Doctor Garrett at the fertility clinic and have a baby on my own."

The ladies laughed together, but Chloe couldn't miss the note of seriousness in what Gracie had said. It made her pause for thought. Ever since she and her mom had left Texas, they'd lived on the bare minimum. She'd dreamed of having enough money one day to be able to go shopping for groceries without having to count every penny. To live like a Wingate, basically. But it seemed money brought its own problems, too. It was a side of things she hadn't really considered before.

It was late afternoon when she and Beth returned to the Wingate estate after what had turned into a truly lovely afternoon with Gracie. The longer she spent with the women, the more she realized, all differences in their upbringings aside, they could truly be friends.

Chloe had never had a large group of friends growing up. Her mom had been relying on her to make something of her life, so she had done whatever she could academically and on the track to ensure she'd be eligible for scholarships, which meant she hadn't had the time to socialize like her peers. But an afternoon like this one? Well, it had served to remind her that her life hadn't been as balanced as it probably should have been. As they started up the long driveway, Chloe turned to Beth, who was driving.

"Thank you so much for including me today. It was really lovely to meet Gracie and to spend time with you both."

Beth gave her a big smile in return. "You're welcome. I know your visit with us hasn't been under the best circumstances, but I can see how much you mean to Miles. You're important to him. I want you to feel included, and I look forward to getting to know you better. You can never have too many friends in this world, right?"

Chloe smiled in return and looked out the front window of the car feeling a whole lot lighter than she had since she'd arrived here. She was fitting in. She was being accepted as a part of Miles's life, and it felt marvelous. There was one dark spot on the horizon, though. The way she'd engineered their meeting. She had to come clean with him and face the consequences of that. She owed it to him. He'd been nothing but up-front with her and he deserved her honesty.

As they neared the house, she spied a different car parked out front. The vehicle was dusty with road grime, as if it had done some miles before getting here.

"That looks like my aunt Piper's car. We weren't expecting her," Beth mused aloud as she pulled up next to the other vehicle.

They got out of the car and Chloe immediately spied the infant car seat secured in the back. Just as she did so, the front door opened, and a young woman holding a small boy, who couldn't have been more than about four, stood in the doorway.

"Oh my! Harley! Daniel! You're home!" Beth cried.

Chloe watched as Beth ran up the stairs and enveloped her little sister and her nephew in a big welcoming hug. The two women greeted one another with genuine affection. Another, slightly older woman joined them, and Beth squealed with joy and hugged her warmly, too. Chloe spotted the newcomer's resemblance to Ava almost immediately. She must be the aunt that Beth had mentioned lived in Dallas. When she'd spoken of her, it had been with much warmth and love. More so than when she spoke of her own mother. Beth turned back to Chloe and gestured for her to come on and meet everyone.

"Chloe, come up and meet Harley and her son, Daniel. And this is my aunt, Piper Holloway."

Chloe proffered her hand and smiled at each of

the women as she drew up in front of them. "Hi, I'm Chloe Fitzgerald. A friend of Miles's. Lovely to meet you."

"Does Mom know you're back?" Beth asked her little sister.

"Not yet, and I'm not in a hurry to cross paths with her, so our visit here is short. Piper picked me up in Dallas and brought me down, but I'll be staying with an old friend back in Royal."

Beth wore a small frown on her face. "It would have been wonderful to have you here."

"I know, but you know what things are like between Mom and me. I don't want to expose Daniel to that any more than necessary. But I hope to see a lot of you, though. I'm going to need your help."

"Anything," Beth said quickly. "I'm just so thrilled to see you. You've heard about the mess that's going on."

"Yes, I gathered things were bad when Mom called me in Thailand to tell me the income stream from WinJet to Zest had been frozen. It's why I came straight back. I need to find alternative donors and quickly before it starts to impact on the work Zest does. But we had a good flight back to the States and then on to Dallas, didn't we, Daniel?"

The little boy shyly nodded, then turned his face back into his mother's neck.

"He's a little jet-lagged," Harley explained. "Or he'd be talking all our ears off."

"And I was overdue a visit so I offered to drive them from Dallas. It made for a good opportunity to catch up." Piper said. "Besides, there's a new artist just outside of Royal I'm hoping to persuade to give me an exclusive showing at my gallery."

Beth turned to Chloe with a laugh. "Piper has an art gallery in Dallas. We like to tell everyone it's her substitute husband."

Piper chuckled. "Hey, with my gallery I have everything just the way I like it. No crumbs on the breakfast bar in the morning and no socks on the bedroom floor. I'm quite satisfied with my life just the way it is, thank you."

Chloe could see the genuine affection that wove these women together and felt a pang of envy. Even though she wasn't estranged from her mom, they'd never had the kind of relationship the Wingate sisters appeared to have with their aunt. While none of the Wingate children appeared to be emotionally close to their mother, it looked as though they had a strong surrogate in Piper Holloway.

They all went inside and gathered in the family room. There were a few toys already scattered on the floor, as well as a couple of children's books on the coffee table that hadn't been there before. Chloe could see the other women were itching to catch up together, so she suggested she mind Daniel for a bit so they could spend some time alone. At first, Harley looked a little dubious.

"Chloe is an elementary school teacher," Beth filled in for Harley. "Daniel will be quite safe with her, I'm sure."

"Honestly, I miss my class kids so it would be a delight to spend some time with him," Chloe said.

Once Harley had explained she'd just be in another room nearby with his aunts, Daniel accepted that he was being left with Chloe. She kicked off her shoes and joined him on the carpet, helping him put together a wooden track on which he could roll the toy cars he'd brought home with him. She lost track of time and was startled to hear the front door slam closed and the sound of footsteps coming toward them. Chloe looked up to see Miles with a quizzical expression on his face.

"Uncle Miles!" Daniel shouted.

The little boy scrambled to his feet and launched himself at his uncle from about six feet away. To his credit, Miles dropped the briefcase he'd been carrying and caught his nephew in his arms and whirled the giggling child in a circle. Chloe watched him with the boy and felt something shift inside her. What would it be like, she wondered, if the scenario was different and it was *her* child running to his or her daddy. And just like that, Chloe knew she had fallen even harder in love with Miles Wingate.

Thirteen

Miles looked over his nephew's head at the woman sprawled on the floor amongst the toys. She looked just as comfortable there as she had at his side at the engagement party last weekend. More so, in fact. Seeing her like this made him appreciate that there were so many more facets to Chloe than he realized. He'd never gone out with anyone before who didn't think twice about getting down to a child's level and simply having fun with them.

"Miles!" Harley squealed from the side door and came rushing through the room to give her brother a big hug.

Miles flung an arm around his younger sibling and squeezed tight. He'd seen Harley six months ago when he'd been on a business trip to Bangkok.

"Hey, I didn't expect to see you back home, too," he said.

"Piper brought me through from Dallas. She's here, also."

"You didn't mention anything about coming home this year when I saw you last. Is everything okay?"

"Just this wretched business with WinJet. You know they're the primary donor to my charity, Zest. With the freeze, Zest's funding has been locked up, too. I need to drum up new funding to tide us over until this whole mess is cleared up. Is that what you're here for, too? To help with the WinJet crisis?"

Harley looked up at Miles in adoration, and he felt the old familiar twang of pride she'd always managed to imbue in him. His other three siblings were all older, and the twins had always been tight-knit as they all grew up. But Harley had always seen Miles as her knight in shining armor. Cute most of the time. A little less so when he'd started dating and she'd taken it upon herself to start vetting his girlfriends.

"Something like that," he acknowledged. "Although my hands have been tied with the freeze, much like yours back in Thailand, I imagine."

"It's so darn frustrating, isn't it? We're just trying to do good things, make a living, help others to make theirs. I don't know why anyone would be working so hard to discredit us."

"Well, hopefully that will become clearer soon." Miles set Daniel down onto his feet and ruffled the little boy's hair. "He's grown since I saw him last.

But you haven't. Have you lost weight? Are you look-ing after yourself okay?"

"Don't you start," Harley said with a laugh. "I'm doing just fine. C'mon Daniel, let's go to the kitchen to find something to eat. Are you hungry?"

"Yes, please!" the little boy answered and put his hand in his mother's. As he passed Chloe, he gave her a shy smile and a wave with his free hand. "Thank you for playing with me."

"Anytime, Daniel. I enjoyed it," Chloe answered with a warm smile.

There was definitely something about her that made everything in Miles ease and relax. He flopped down next to her on the carpet.

"Nice job on the racetrack," he said, gesturing to the convoluted road Chloe and Daniel had ob-viously built together around the furniture in the room. "I had no idea you were so adept at playing with boys' toys."

Chloe arched a brow at him. "Toys are toys. Gen-der doesn't enter into it."

"I consider myself duly chastened," Miles an-swered playfully.

"As your punishment, you can help me tidy this away. I'm sure when Ava gets back, she'd prefer to see her family room looking its usual pristine self."

Chloe went on all fours and began to disassemble the train track and stack it into the box it came from. Distracted momentarily by her pert derriere, Miles was slow to join her.

"Well, come on!" she said in exasperation.

"Yes, ma'am."

Once the room was back to its regular condition, they went up to their bedroom. Miles flopped down backward on the bed and heaved a big sigh.

"Bad day?" Chloe asked.

"Not a great one. I'm still parsing through the data I put on a hard drive prior to the freeze, but it hasn't revealed much, so far. I feel like I'm this close." He held his thumb and forefinger close together in the air. "But something is eluding me. Whoever did this knows the Wingate business systems inside and out. I've got my team in Chicago working on improving overall security for the entire corporation. It just frustrates me because this all could have been avoided if they'd listened to me earlier about their IT security."

Chloe sat down next to him on the bed. "I'm sorry this is proving so tough for you."

"Hey, it's not your fault. How about you? Did you have a good day?"

She smiled down at him. "Yeah, I did. I got to know Gracie a little better. She's quite a woman. I'm glad Beth has her support. And your aunt Piper seems lovely, too. And she's so close to Beth and Harley."

"Yeah, Piper is the mother figure we never had growing up. We all love her to bits. And Beth is brilliant at what she does and even better at choosing people to help her who are equally as strong. Hopefully she can pull some magic out of a hat for Harley, too."

"Harley seems nice," Chloe commented as she lay partway down beside him and started stroking his chest with one hand.

"Harley is one of life's truly good people. I think that by the time she was born, all the snark had been bred out of us, leaving her only what was sweetness and light."

"That's such a cute way to portray her. You do know she's a grown woman with a child," she teased him.

"Yeah, I know. We were all shocked when she announced she was pregnant with Daniel. She was only nineteen when he was born, and she refused to tell any of us who his father is. I think Sebastian and Sutton were on the verge of organizing a lynch mob. But she's done an amazing job of raising him on her own, and she's taught him a lot about compassion and sharing, too."

"He's a darling kid. I really liked being with him."

Miles rolled onto his side and looked Chloe in the eye. "Have you ever thought about having kids?"

"Of course. I love kids. I always hoped I'd have two or three of my own one day. When I was with the right man, of course. I know a lot of strong women, like your sister, tackle raising a child on their own, but having spent most of my life without a father figure, I would prefer to have an involved and present father there for my children."

Miles knew it was still early days in their relationship but it gave him a deep sense of satisfaction to hear that Chloe's views on parenting were so similar to his own. Wanting a family and raising that family with a woman he considered his equal and enjoyed having by his side was part of the reason he'd bought the three-story town house he had back in Chicago. There was a yard out back; they'd be close to the Park for bike rides and walks. And for everything else they could always come back to Texas.

This business with WinJet and his family was a temporary thing, he was sure. While it looked bad right now, he had no doubt that eventually they'd be cleared of the charges that had been laid against them. Until that happened, though, he was bound to support his family. And, while his own personal wealth and his business wasn't affected by this, yet, he couldn't honestly think of or plan for a future until the present was more secure. But when it was, he was looking forward to exploring that concept of the future with the woman lying here with him on the bed.

And speaking of the woman lying on the bed, her hand, which had been massaging the muscles of his chest had begun a slow, but determined, trajectory to the waistband of his trousers. Instantly his flesh leaped to attention. It seemed that no matter the external stressors in his life, one thing remained constant. His powerful attraction to Chloe Fitzgerald.

"Is that linen you're wearing?" he asked her.

A puzzled frown appeared between her eyes. "Yes, why?"

"That stuff creases badly—you should probably take it off."

"Is that right?" she purred.

Chloe withdrew her hand and sat up on the bed, reaching for the tab of her zipper.

"Here, let me," he said, also rising to a sitting position.

He brushed her hand away and reached for the tab, then ever so slowly lowered it, inch by inch exposing smooth honey-colored skin. Then he bent forward, and with his other hand, brushed her hair off her neck and placed his lips at her nape. He felt the tremor that rippled through her body in response to his touch. Emboldened, he lowered the zipper farther, placing kisses on each vertebra of her back as he did so.

It only took a moment to push the garment off her shoulders and down to her waist. Miles stood and pulled her to her feet, letting the dress slip to the floor in a heap and leaving her standing there in pristine white lingerie that was anything but innocent. Behind the sheer lace of the cups of her bra he saw her sweet pink nipples tighten, and he reached for her, thumbing those taut peaks through the fabric.

"Stay there," he directed as he swiftly undid the buttons of his shirt and tugged it free of his waistband before shedding it and throwing it down beside him.

He stepped forward and wrapped her in his arms, bending his head to hers. She lifted her lips in response and he kissed her, his tongue gently probing past her lips to dance against her tongue before withdrawing. The taste of her, hell, everything about her, intoxicated him on every level. And he couldn't get enough.

He reached for the clasp of her bra and, with the deft fingers of one hand, unsnapped the hooks. The confection of fabric fell free and he gingerly tugged it off her, exposing her small perfect breasts to his gaze. He didn't waste another second. He bent his head to her breast, taking one nipple in his mouth and rolling the tight bud with his tongue. Chloe moaned and clutched at his head, holding him there as he kissed and licked and sucked her. He could spend an eternity with Chloe and still never have enough of her.

He carefully walked her backward to the bed and guided her down on the covers before tugging her panties off and tossing them on the growing pile of attire on the floor. Then, he shucked off the rest of his clothes and joined her on the bed. He lay beside her, propped up on one arm while he traced the glorious feminine lines of her body with his other hand.

"You know, these past couple of weeks have really opened my eyes."

She writhed beneath his touch and her eyes met his. "They have?"

"Yeah. I can see that being with the right person can make anything bearable. I think you could be *my* right person, Chloe."

For the briefest moment she looked conflicted and she briefly averted her gaze. When she looked back at him, her eyes shone with unshed tears. "Oh, Miles. That's a beautiful thing to say. Thank you. I feel honored that you feel that way about me, and I have to be completely honest with you and admit I never expected to want to make your world right or to need you as much as I do. But I do."

He didn't know how to tell her what her words meant to him. Instead, he showed her with his body just how much *she* meant to him. He moved over her and settled between her legs and relished the feel of her hands as they stroked his back and clutched at his buttocks, urging him to take her and drive them both to the pinnacle of their need for one another. So he did, and as he entered her body he knew he'd found the place he needed to be—not just now, but forever—and it was with her.

It was a couple of days later, and Chloe had gone riding with Harley and Daniel, when his mother asked him if he could meet with her and Keith Cooper for lunch at the club. Ava, it seemed, was determined for everyone around them to see that things within the family were strictly business as usual and even though the news had not yet broken about the asset freeze at WinJet, Miles knew it wouldn't be long before it was front page news.

The family had spent many hours in meetings discussing the best ways to manage the impending fallout. To that end, Zeke had been working overtime with a trusted handful of staff in the marketing department. Miles could only hope his cousin's preemptive damage control would do its job.

He'd been catching up on Steel Security business

from the estate today, and as he drove out to the club, he decided there was little he could still do from here that was any concrete help to his family, other than showing a united front. He'd discuss it with Chloe, but he felt it was definitely time for them to head home. He knew she had classroom prep and shopping to do for the rapidly approaching start of the school year, too.

Miles smiled a little to himself as he parked his car and sauntered to the club's main entrance. In the last two days he'd felt closer to Chloe than ever. Admitting to his feelings for her—it was something he'd never done before with another woman. In fact, he'd begun to wonder if he'd ever find the right gal for him, but there she was and all because of an accidental meeting in the park.

He spied his mom and Uncle Keith at their usual table in the restaurant and walked toward them. They were talking earnestly, heads bent together. Miles didn't quite know how he felt about the development of his mom's relationship with the man who used to be his father's best friend. He knew Beth wasn't completely happy about it, either. But his mom wasn't easily fooled, and if she found comfort in Keith Cooper's almost constant presence by her side, then so be it. Goodness only knew she'd been faithful and loyal to her husband for all the years of their marriage. Maybe it was his own newfound joy in love that was coloring his way of thinking, but if Uncle Keith made his mom happy, then Miles could accept it, even if he'd never been particularly fond of the man. Besides, if anyone could keep a rein on the man's temper, it was Ava.

His mom looked up and gave him a brief wave, beckoning him over to join them. At the table, he shook hands with Cooper and bent to place a kiss on his mother's cheek before sitting down.

"You two look as if you're in cahoots about something," Miles said as he picked up his water glass and took a long pull at the icy liquid.

"Miles, darling, Keith has brought something to my attention that I think you really need to hear."

It was the use of the word *darling* that did it. His mother wasn't the kind of person to use terms of endearment.

"Oh?" Miles said and looked straight at the older man across the table. "And that would be?"

"No need to get your hackles up, boy," Cooper said. "Your mother and I are merely looking after your interests."

His proprietary tone when he mentioned Ava and calling him a boy irritated Miles on a level he didn't want to study too carefully. Instead, he put his game face on. The one he used when he was about to deliver serious news to one of his clients about their safety.

"Perhaps you'd like to enlighten me?"

"Now, Miles, don't be defensive. Keith, tell him what you told me about Chloe."

Chloe? What did she have to do with Cooper?

"Yes, Uncle Keith, How about you tell me."

Miles kept his barely banked irritation firmly under control.

"Well," Cooper started, reaching out a hand and taking hold of Ava's as if to comfort her. "Your dad wasn't always the best kind of man when it came to business."

"Tell me something I don't know," Miles bit out.

His father's approach to business and Miles's ethics had never been on the same page. It was what had driven him to make his own place in the world thirteen hundred miles away from where he'd been born and bred.

Cooper nodded his head in acknowledgment. "There was a situation a little under twenty years ago where Trent behaved particularly badly. He entered into a verbal agreement with an acquaintance of his who was in the business of making aircraft seats and supplying them to private jet manufacturers."

Miles began to feel a creeping sense of uneasiness at the tale.

"Sounds like a reasonable thing to do."

"Well, yes, it would have been. Except when this acquaintance of his invested heavily in the materials to supply WinJet exclusively, Trent decided to pull the plug on the arrangement. As they'd never entered into a written contract and only agreed to their partnership on a handshake, the poor guy didn't have a leg to stand on. His suppliers started demanding payment for the stock he'd bought in anticipation of the WinJet job, which he obviously couldn't pay for and he went bankrupt.

"Trent just stood by and watched a man, who'd trusted him, dig himself deeper and deeper in debt, and when the guy was forced to walk away from his business, your father swooped in and bought the remains of the company out from under him and amalgamated it into WinJet, where it remains today."

Miles pursed his lips and considered what Keith had told him. None of it came as any surprise. It was just the kind of underhanded thing he knew his father was capable of. The man had always wanted to win at any cost and damn the consequences. Miles had long believed his father was devoid of any social conscience and had often wondered how his mother, who'd once been heavily involved in philanthropic works, had coped with that. But then again, he rationalized, maybe that's why she'd worked so hard for charity—to offset his father's less stellar attributes.

"I don't see what that has to do with Chloe."

"I'm getting to it. Just listen. After being let down by the very man who'd promised to grow his business and being made bankrupt, then seeing his company sell to the one person who could have prevented his downfall, the poor guy committed suicide." Keith sighed heavily. "I went to his funeral. I'll never forget seeing his wife and daughter. They were bereft. They'd not only lost their husband and father, they'd lost *everything*. He'd cashed up life insurances and cleared out his bank accounts all in a desperate attempt to keep his business afloat and to pay back his creditors. His name was John—" he paused before continuing "—John Fitzgerald. And his daughter's name is Chloe."

Miles felt his stomach drop and the chill of arctic waters ran through his veins. His father had cheated Chloe's dad?

"Why didn't you say anything sooner?" he ground out when he could trust himself to speak. Miles looked at his mother, who looked equally shocked.

"I didn't know," she uttered in a strangled whisper. "I would have done something, anything. I had no idea Trent had done something so vile. He never told me about the initial agreement, but I remember him being very smug about acquiring the aircraft seat manufacturing plant and absorbing it into WinJet."

"And I wasn't certain until now," Keith said, patting Ava comfortingly on her hand. "I thought Chloe looked familiar at the Fourth of July barbecue. You even heard me say as much. But she denied ever meeting any of us before she met you. Remember? So my questions to you, Miles, are, what's her agenda and why is she keeping her family's earlier involvement with us a secret?"

Fourteen

Chloe was rubbing her horse down and laughing at something Daniel had just said when she heard foot-steps approaching the stables. The smile was still on her face when she looked up and saw Miles in the doorway, but it soon died away as she saw the expression in his eyes. He was angry. Furiously, undeniably angry. So much so that he barely even acknowledged his sister or his nephew, who both looked nervously between him and Chloe before making their good-byes and heading up to the house.

"Is something wrong?" Chloe asked, her fingers clutching tight around the currycomb in her hand as if her life depended on it.

"Who are you? Really?" Miles demanded.

Waves of rage billowed off him, and Chloe swallowed against the knot of fear that now constricted her throat.

"I… I'm Chloe Fitzgerald. Just like I always told you. I never lied about who I am."

"Chloe Fitzgerald. Daughter of Loretta and John Fitzgerald of Royal, Texas."

Her legs began to shake. *He knew?* How? What had happened?

"Miles, please. I was going to tell you. I wanted to tell you so many times."

"Really? We've been virtually glued at the hip for the past two and a half weeks. Living side by side, sleeping together, making love—"

His voice broke on the last two words, and Chloe felt her heart begin to shatter into a million tiny pieces. He dragged in a breath and continued.

"I trusted you. I brought you here. To my family home. And you—" His voice broke off and he shook his head. "I don't even know what kind of agenda you had. Can you imagine how it felt to have someone else inform me as to your true identity? You violated every level of trust I placed in you. I can't believe I was that blind. Did it give you a good laugh to deceive me? And, tell me, our first meeting—it was a sham right from the start, wasn't it?"

"Miles, I'm sorry—"

He put up a hand, halting her in whatever she'd been about to say next.

"Don't. Just don't bother lying to me anymore. I want you out of here. I've arranged a car for you to the airport and a charter flight to get you home. After that, you're on your own."

He turned to leave and she shot across the short distance that separated them and grabbed hold of his arm.

"And you're just dumping me like that? Without hearing me out? Without trying to understand any of this from my point of view?"

"Sure looks that way," he said harshly, and shook off her hand.

"Miles, I love you."

"Oh, don't go making this any worse than it already is. I think we've already established you're a liar."

"But I haven't lied to you. I might have omitted to tell you everything about my family's background, but I haven't lied."

"So you're saying our meeting was a coincidence?"

"No." She shook her head. "I'm not. I did force our meeting. I had this ridiculous idea that I could somehow insert myself into your life and learn what I could about your family with a view to using what I learned to somehow help my mom get her life back on track. She's lived with the misery of knowing your father's actions drove my father to suicide all these years. She wanted some kind of payback. And me? Well, I wanted my mom back."

"Payback? Why not call it what it is. Revenge." His voice was cold, and the expression on his face told her it tasted as bad in his mouth as admitting it to him had tasted in hers. "I can't believe I was so stupid as to fall for you."

She felt each word as if it was a stab to her heart.

"Miles, I never expected to fall in love with you, either."

"Oh, so that makes what you did better? I don't think so. You've not only betrayed me, you've betrayed my whole family. I've said my piece. The car will be here in fifteen minutes. Make sure you're in it when it leaves."

He started to walk away from her again, and she knew she had only one last chance to try and make this right.

"You have no idea what it's like. To see your father crumble from the strong and healthy man who loved and supported you to someone who just sat in a chair and wept constantly. I was eight years old. Eight! It terrified me. And when he decided it was easier to take his life than to face rebuilding it with my mom and me, I was the one who found him. It was…horrifying.

"And then my mom fell apart. She'd held it together through the worst of the company stuff, but after he died she lost it. She still hasn't recovered. Yes, she's bitter and, yes, that bitterness transferred to me. Have I spent every day since my father killed himself wondering if one day I'd come home and discover my mom had done the same thing? Of course, I have."

Chloe paused and dashed away the tears of anguish and grief that stung her eyes before taking a deep breath and continuing in a fiercely controlled voice. "And did we see your family lose anything while we lost it all?" She shook her head. "You lost nothing. Your father could have reached out at any time and helped us, or, here's an idea, honored his original agreement with my father. But he chose not to. So I grew up hating your family—all of you. And when the news came about the fire and the failed safety inspections, well, I saw an opportunity to exploit your misery and I took it.

"But I never expected to discover you were not like your father. I never expected to love you."

Miles stood there—immovable, expressionless— as she spoke so passionately. As she laid her heart bare to him.

"Are you done?" he gritted out.

She could no longer speak. Her eyes flooded with persistent tears, and her throat completely closed as a massive sob rose from deep within and choked her. And then he walked away.

Chloe couldn't remember how she traversed the distance between the stables and the house, but she found herself in their room, her suitcase opened on the bed, and piling the items she'd brought with her into it. The tears had stopped, but the raw pain of loss clawed at her from deep inside. It couldn't end this way, she kept telling herself. But it had.

She didn't even bother changing her clothes. She knew he wanted her out of here and that's what she had to do. Once she was packed and had double-checked she hadn't left anything behind, she grabbed her handbag and her suitcase and went downstairs. Ava was just coming in through the front door with Keith Cooper as Chloe reached the bottom of the stairs.

"Chloe? You're leaving us?"

"Miles has asked me to go," she said stiffly. "But before I do, I just wanted to apologize to you. To your whole family, really. I didn't disclose who I was, and by omission I have lied to you all about my intentions toward your family. I didn't expect to like you all so much, much less fall in love with Miles. But I can't deny that I had an agenda when I met him. My feelings for Miles, now, are true. I only hope that someday he can forgive me for what I've done."

"Oh, Chloe."

Unexpectedly, Ava rushed toward her and enveloped Chloe in a brief hug. Chloe held herself stiffly. Unable to accept the solace Miles's mother offered because if she did, she would crumble into a thousand pieces and not be able to move again. She had to say her goodbyes. She had to leave. Not to do so would be in direct contradiction of his wishes and, above all else, his wishes were paramount.

Thankfully, Ava let her go and, with a nod to Keith Cooper, Chloe continued out the front door and to the car that had just pulled up in the driveway.

"Ms. Fitzgerald?" the driver asked as he got out of the car to open the back door for her and take her case.

"Yes."

She got in the rear of the car and the driver closed

the door. The dull thud a final knell to the hopes she'd begun to nurture that she could have a future with Miles. Once the driver had stowed her case in the trunk, he took his seat behind the wheel.

"To the airport, right?"

"Yes, to the airport."

She didn't even bother looking back. This was the last time she would leave Texas. The first had been painful and full of uncertainty, but this was so much worse. Because this time she felt as though she was leaving a vital part of her behind. A part that she would never recover again.

By the time she landed in Chicago it was getting late. She texted her mom from the airport to let her know she was back. It took her just over an hour and a half, using public transport, to get to her home. Despite her mother's frequent visits, the house smelled musty, but Chloe locked the front door behind her, dropped her bags in the hallway and then went straight to her bathroom and turned on the shower.

She could still smell the scent of her horse on her clothing as she stripped off and stepped into the shower stall. And there, she let go of all the pent-up misery of the past several hours. It was ages later before she could summon the energy to wash her body and her hair. Even longer before she had the strength to turn off the water and dry herself.

Exhausted by grief, she tumbled naked into her bed and closed her eyes, willing herself to sleep, but all she could think about was the shock and betrayal she'd seen on Miles's face. Knowing she'd hurt him so badly was like being flayed with a whip and left her entire body sore and aching. She thought she was done crying but as she flipped and flopped on the bed, she realized that her pillow was now sodden with the steady stream of tears that simply would not let up.

So she curled into a ball and she let herself cry and wail and howl. And in the end, none of it made any difference. She was still alone. And she'd devastated the only man she'd ever truly loved.

"Chloe? I know you're in there, honey. I'll let myself in if you don't come to the door."

Chloe woke to the sound of her mother's fist battering on her front door. She dragged herself from her bed and wrapped herself in a robe before staggering to the door and opening it. Bright sunlight streamed through the open portal, temporarily blinding her, and she put a hand up to shade her eyes.

"Oh, honey. What happened?" Loretta asked, stepping across the threshold and kicking the door closed behind her while enveloping her daughter in her arms.

Chloe tried to hold herself together, the way she always had for her mom. Since her father's death she'd learned that her role was to comfort her mom, not the other way around, but right now she lacked the energy to hide her hurt. Instead, she leaned right into Loretta's softer frame and put her arms around her mother's waist.

"I fell in love, Momma. And I broke his heart and then he broke mine."

"Oh, my darling girl. I'm so sorry."

Her mother hugged her tight and didn't move, didn't say a thing. Just held her. The tears cleared more quickly this time and, once she'd stopped, Loretta led her into the sitting room and pushed her down onto the couch.

"I'll go make us some coffee and get you something to eat."

"I'm not hungry, Momma, truly."

"I'm going to fix you something and you're going to eat it. Then you're going to tell me everything."

"I don't have any food in the house," Chloe protested.

"And why do you think I came around this morning?" Loretta asked as she moved around the room opening windows. "I got you some groceries. If you'd given me notice that you were coming home, I'd have aired the place out and had some food in the fridge for you for when you arrived. But as it stands, I'm glad you didn't, because you'd have just borne this alone, wouldn't you?"

Chloe couldn't deny it. She'd spent the last nineteen years learning to suck up whatever bothered her and, while this was more monumental than anything she'd endured before, she would have tried to shield her mom from this, too.

"It makes no difference. Telling you won't change the outcome."

"A problem shared is a problem halved, honey. Remember that."

Chloe cracked the weakest of smiles as her mom espoused one of her dad's favorite sayings. He also used to say that happiness shared was doubled, but Chloe didn't know if she'd ever feel happy again. She sat back on the couch and watched as her mom put away a couple of bags of groceries and then put a pan on the stovetop. Soon the air was redolent with the aroma of fresh coffee, toasted bread and fried eggs with bacon. The scents of her childhood, she realized as Loretta loaded everything on a tray and brought it through to her.

Despite her protestation that she wasn't hungry, Chloe did her best to eat the simple meal her mom had prepared for her. To her surprise, once she started, she couldn't stop until it was all gone. She was on her second cup of coffee when her mother sat down next to her and patted her on the leg.

"Now, tell me everything," she urged her daughter.

So Chloe did. She unloaded everything—well, the G-rated version anyway—that she'd said and done with Miles right up until he'd ordered her out of his life. To her credit, Loretta didn't once interrupt, and when Chloe was finished speaking she merely shook her head.

"It was like that with your daddy and me. Falling in love hard and fast. High emotions. They're exhilarating and exhausting all at the same time, aren't they?"

Chloe just nodded. She knew her parents had had a whirlwind courtship, but she hadn't wanted to ask her mom too much by the time she was old enough to show an interest, because doing so would only cause her mom more pain.

"I'm sorry, Momma. I failed you."

"No, don't you dare say that! You haven't failed me at all."

"But I didn't get the revenge we'd both talked about for so long. When it came down to it, I couldn't do it."

"And I'm glad you didn't, to be honest. When you called me and told me that you weren't going forward, I'll admit I was mad at you for not following through with your plans, and I was determined to finish off what you started." Releasing a pent-up breath, Loretta admitted, "But then I got to thinking, and I realized it shouldn't have ever been your fight. It was mine. Realizing that made me see I'd failed you as a parent all these years. I put unrealistic pressures and expectations on you your whole life and, you know, to be totally honest, it's all credit to you that you're the incredible human being you are.

"I also realized that I've been selfish for quite long enough."

"No, Momma, never selfish," Chloe protested.

"Yes, honey. I can see that now. I was so wrapped in my own grief and all we'd lost with your daddy dying, and I harbored a fair amount of anger toward him, as well, for leaving us to deal with it all on our own. I just didn't see how much you needed me, too. I took all the support you gave me and I expected more. That was wrong—and that's going to change from here on in. I promise.

"When you told me about the drugs and the DEA, I knew that making that news public would be crippling to the Wingates. I wanted to do that more than anything, to bring them to their knees the way Trent Wingate brought your father to his. But I also realized that doing so would hurt you, too, and I've hurt you enough, my darling girl. It's time I stopped living in the past. Time I took control of me and my life and let you live yours."

"Oh, Momma, I don't ever want to be without you," Chloe said fervently.

"And you won't be. But *I'll* be the mother from this moment forward. You will be able to depend on me as should always have been your right. And I want you to reach out to your young man once he's had a few days to calm down. You both deserve a bright future together."

Chloe shook her head slowly. "I don't think he'll ever forgive me for this. I betrayed him in the worst possible way."

"Keep the faith. If your love for one another is as strong as you believe it is, it'll work out eventually."

"I hope so."

"Believe it, honey. True love never dies. It takes a hit sometimes, but it *never* goes away."

Chloe watched as her mom stacked their cups

on the tray together with her breakfast plate and took it through to the kitchen. She wondered if her mom was right.

Fifteen

Miles was like a dead man walking. A snarly one at that. Everyone, even Daniel, had kept a wide berth since he'd sent Chloe home. Miles had been back in Royal for three weeks now, and they'd been both the worst and the best of his life. Heavy on the worst, he told himself.

Chloe had been gone only three days, and while he told himself, frequently, that was a good thing, he found himself missing her so badly it had become a physical ache. He'd avoided his family over the past weekend and had spent most of his waking hours at the head office of Wingate Enterprises working on running the beta version of the new IT security system his team back in Chicago had designed for the company. So far it had been running perfectly and at this rate, in another few days, he'd be able to head back to Chicago and be satisfied that any surprise glitches could be managed remotely from there.

But that didn't stop the hurt that reverberated through his every waking moment. He let himself back into the house and headed for the stairs up to his room. It was late and the house was quiet, but he was surprised when he saw his mother come from the main sitting room.

"Miles, we need to talk," she said firmly.

"Not now, Mom. I'm tired and I need my bed."

"What you need is a good talking-to, and you're going to get it whether it's down here in the sitting room or up in your bedroom if I have to follow you there. And don't think you can lock the door on me. This is *my* house, remember? I hold all the keys. So, which is it to be?"

Ava put her hands on her hips and stared at him, awaiting his response. Miles sighed in frustration, knowing she'd darn well follow him upstairs and to his room if he tried to avoid her.

"Fine," he said with ill humor. "Let's get it over with."

"Thank you," Ava murmured, preceding him into the sitting room.

She settled on one of the leather wingback chairs by a picture window that looked down the hill and toward the lake, although it was pitch-dark out now and even under the scant moonlight there was little to be seen. Ava gestured for him to take the other seat, and he threw himself down and leaned forward, forearms resting on his knees, hands clasped together and head bowed in acquiescence. He was startled when he felt his mother's hand on his hair. Even more so when her fingers shifted to his chin and forced him to raise his face toward her.

"Miles, I hate seeing you like this."

"What? Tired? Once I'm satisfied with the new IT system I'll get plenty of rest again. But it's vital everything is running properly before I leave because I don't plan on being back anytime soon."

"I'm sorry to hear that. I had hoped, in these years since your father's death, you would come to see this as a place you are always welcome to come home to. That you might even consider moving back to Royal, even if not onto the estate."

He shook his head, staring at her in disbelief. "No, that's not going to happen."

"I know your father was hard on you, but—"

"*Hard* on me? He took every opportunity to let me know I was a disappointment to him. Hardly the actions of a good man or a good father."

"Everything he did, he did for us," Ava said in fierce defense.

"Everything? Really, Mom? Even driving a man to suicide? I don't know how it made you feel to hear that the other day, but it made me sick to my stomach and ashamed to even bear the name Wingate. I can't believe that even now, knowing what kind of man he truly was, that you still continue to stand by him or that you continue to mourn him."

His mother's face bore a mask of pain for a moment, but she pulled herself up straight and her features cleared.

"One can forgive much if the love is real, Miles. I want you to think about that. I know you sent Chloe away after discovering her background but I'd like you to consider just how different you are from your father right now. Isn't that exactly what he would have done in the same situation?"

Miles flinched as if she'd slapped him. "Don't go there, Mom. I'm nothing like him. *Nothing!*"

"Don't you realize it, yet? The harder you try not to be like someone, often the more like them you become." He stared at her in stony silence but allowed her to continue.

"You have all the good of your father. Be careful you don't develop the bad along with it." She released a quavering breath, and when she spoke again, her voice rang with emotion.

"Yes, I know he wore two masks. I know he could be ruthless at times, and while your father capitalized on another man's unhappiness, he did everything he could to ensure that you children always had everything you ever needed whether it was the roof over your heads or the educations you undertook. He used to watch you sleep at night, when you were babies, and he'd share with me his dreams for our future, for the empire he wanted to build so that none of us would ever want for anything. He loved you all in his way."

Miles wanted to refute his mother's words. To tell her she'd viewed her late husband through rose-colored glasses and that the man had been a monster, not some gallant hero forging a life for his family. But deep down, he knew that, faults and all, that's exactly what his father had done. It didn't mean that Miles's feelings toward him changed one iota, and he could live with that. What he couldn't live with, however, was his mom thinking he was just like the man who'd fathered him.

Ava continued. "Miles, I need to be honest with you. I wasn't thrilled when I saw you'd brought someone home with you, especially under the circumstances we're facing. But I could see that she was special to you and, the longer you two stayed, the more I could see how right Chloe is for you. She brought out a softness I haven't seen in you since you were a little boy. Softness your father drummed out of you. Yes, he shouldn't have done that, but you're an adult now. You make your choices. You decide how you treat people, how you'll let them treat you.

"I know how hard you've worked to build your own empire and you've done an outstanding job. But—and you have to admit I'm right here—it's a lonely life managing everything on your own. Chloe loves you. Even a blind man could see that. Give her another chance. Don't let the fact she hid her true identity from you banish her from your life forever."

"I trusted her," he said bitterly.

"I know. We all did. And, when you look at the bigger picture, whatever her initial intentions were, she didn't betray that trust. People make mistakes, but I believe she loves you, Miles. The way you deserve to be loved. Wholeheartedly. You need to make this right between the two of you."

"I don't know if I can do that."

"Then maybe you're your father's son after all," she said quietly.

Ava rose from her chair and placed a gentle hand on his shoulder before leaving the room. A cascade of thoughts tumbled through his mind. He thought back to the moment he met Chloe, to his instant visceral reaction to her. To his need to ensure she was okay, and not just medically okay but safely home and fed and cared for. Those weren't his usual reactions on meeting someone. He'd taken her at face value and he'd acted accordingly. Why? She'd admitted she set up the whole thing. Goodness knows how many times she'd lain in wait for him, trying to force a meeting.

But there were no guarantees that even if they'd met that he'd have fallen for her bait and wanted to see more of her. She'd taken a risk but he had the feeling that for all the years of unhappiness she'd endured, she really hadn't thought the whole thing through. And even if Chloe had released any of the information she'd gleaned from his family during her time here, how much damage could that have done to any of them, anyway? Every dirty, nasty, fact would come out eventually. In fact, he was surprised that nothing had leaked already.

Whoever had been trafficking the drugs stood to gain more by besmirching the Wingate family and falsifying their involvement in all this than whatever

Chloe could possibly achieve by sharing details with the media. Which she hadn't done in the end, anyway. Not even after he'd sent her back to Chicago. A truly vindictive woman bent on revenge would have been on the phone to the papers, selling her story to the highest bidder, the moment she was off the property. Maybe even before that. But Chloe hadn't.

Miles got up and faced out the window at the darkness, staring at his reflection in the glass. Right now, he didn't particularly like what he saw. Yes, he was still the same man who always stared back in the mirror when he shaved each day. But his eyes were empty. His soul bleak.

He missed her.

He wanted her.

He had to know if she'd been telling the truth about her feelings for him.

Acknowledging those things didn't make him weak. It made him strong. And what he decided to do about it could make him even stronger.

The next morning, Miles went into the office before dawn. He ran a final check over the beta security system and decided it was time to hand it over. Just to be certain everything was covered, he contacted one of his best analyst/programmers back in Chicago, apologizing for waking her.

"Steph, I need you here on the Texas job. How quickly can you pack and get on a flight?"

He heard her sheets rustle as she obviously got out of bed, soon followed by the sound of fingers clicking on a keyboard.

"Well, I've missed the red-eye but I should be able to be there by three this afternoon. Is that soon enough?"

It would have to be. "Great," Miles said abruptly. "I'll have a car and a driver waiting at the airport for you when you arrive."

"Sure, boss. Um, is everything okay?"

Miles allowed himself to smile for the first time in days. "It's going to be."

Chloe closed her classroom door behind her and made her way out of the building. Normally, she loved this time of year. The anticipation of the classroom filled with new faces. Of the bright young minds waiting to be filled with enthusiasm for learning. But today her feet dragged and her heart lay like a lump of concrete in her chest. She had to pull herself together in the next couple of weeks or she wouldn't be bringing her best to her students or to her love of teaching. But how was she supposed to find joy when, no matter what she did, she couldn't stop thinking about Miles Wingate?

Her mom was doing her best to cheer her up, but there were only so many mother-daughter dates you could fit into a week. Loretta had even suggested Chloe give up the lease on the house and come and live with her again. After relishing her independence all these years, she was shocked to find herself considering it. Yes, the commute to the elementary school where she taught would be longer, but she wouldn't be so darn alone all the time.

She could tell her mom was deeply worried about the cloud of sorrow that hung around Chloe's shoulders. It worried Chloe, too. Even after her father's death she'd managed to keep putting one foot in front of the other. She'd needed to, for her mom's sake. But now it was Momma that was the strong and supportive one, and all Chloe wanted to do was take to her bed, hide under the covers and not come out until her heart didn't hurt so much anymore.

She'd walked to school today, hoping the much-needed exercise might help to lift her mood, but now, it was growing dark out and the idea of walking home didn't hold a great deal of appeal. Still, she squared her shoulders and, with her house keys firmly lodged between the fingers of her right hand, she headed for home.

Chloe hadn't been walking long before she became aware of a vehicle driving toward her. Dark and sleek and all too similar to the one Miles had driven, she felt her stomach lurch as she wondered if it was him. But the car continued on down the street, away from her, and she felt the sharp sting of tears in her eyes as she realized she'd have to be dreaming to think that a man like Miles Wingate would ever forgive her for what she'd done, let alone come and find her.

She dashed the tears away, firmly telling herself to get a grip. She couldn't spend forever moping about. She had a life to live. Kids to teach. Maybe even someone new to fall in love with.

At the thought of allowing herself to get close

to anyone else, her stomach did that weird lurch
again. No, she definitely wasn't ready to consider
that again. Not now and maybe not ever. Everything
was still so raw. Chloe knew she'd done wrong, and
that she had to learn from this and move on. She kept
striding forward, knowing each step took her closer
to home and the chance to lock herself away in her
little house and nurse her wounded soul in private.

The sound of rubber on the road behind her made
her stop in her tracks, her fingers clutching her keys
even tighter than before. A dark shape drew up beside her. Her heart hammered in her chest. The car's
engine was soundless, which was why she hadn't
even heard its approach until it was right there beside her, but she recognized the outline of the sleek
machine. The driver's door was flung open, and the
interior light of the car blazed on, revealing an all
too familiar male figure before he alighted from the
car and stood there, staring at her over the top of the
roof. She felt his presence as if it was an emotional
punch to her midriff. Seeing him standing there sent
her already chaotic emotions into overdrive, leaving
her conflicted and confused.

"We need to talk," Miles said in a low monotone.

She couldn't say why, but instead of leaping at
the opportunity she'd been dreaming of, she just got
mad.

"Why, hello, Chloe. How are you? Did you make
it home from Royal, okay? Oh, lovely, I see you
did. And how are you faring? Well, I hope." Fury
mounted, replacing the miasma of misery she'd been

dwelling on within. "We need to talk, do we? You wouldn't listen to me when I tried to talk to you before. Why the hell should I listen to you now?"

She turned her back on him and kept walking. There was a dull thud of a car door and then the creeping sound of tires on the road as he followed her. The car drew up beside her again and the passenger window rolled down.

"Chloe, please. I'd like to talk."

Every cell in her body was urging her to do as he asked. To actually stop walking and get into that luxury status symbol that he drove, but a perverse imp of self-preservation made her keep putting one foot in front of the other. A couple was walking toward her, and she saw concern painted clearly on both their faces. The man stepped forward.

"Ma'am, are you okay? Is this guy bothering you?" he asked. "Would you like us to call the police?"

"No, it's okay. I know him, I just—"

She just what? She didn't know what she wanted. From the minute she'd left the Wingate estate, she'd wanted Miles. In fact, through every waking moment and almost every sleeping one since, she'd wanted him. She'd wanted what they had to be still in one piece, not shattered and bleeding all over the floor. She'd wanted to feel as if she was a part of him, the way he was indelibly a part of her. She dragged in another breath before speaking to her potential rescuer.

"Thank you for asking. I'll be fine."

And with that, she turned toward Miles's car and

let herself into the passenger side. As he drove the car away from the curb, she forced herself to smile and wave to the couple.

"I appreciate you not making a scene back there," Miles said, keeping his eyes firmly on the road in front of them.

Chloe didn't know what to say so she opted for silence. The moment Miles pulled up outside her house she got out of the car and walked to the front door. She could feel Miles just a few steps behind her. Once they were inside, she gestured to the living room, and he went and sat down on the sofa.

"I'll be back in a moment," she said.

She probably needed more than a moment to gather her thoughts together but with him right here under her roof right this minute, the least she could do was dump her things in her bedroom and then go and wash her hands and face. After leaving her bags on the desk she kept in the corner of her room, she scurried to the bathroom and quickly splashed some cold water on her face.

Chloe regarded her reflection in the mirror. She looked like a wreck. The light summer tan she'd accumulated during the break had faded and a lack of sleep had left her skin and eyes pale and dull. She quickly dried herself off and forced herself to return down the hall to where Miles awaited her.

He hadn't stayed seated. Instead, he was up and pacing the threadbare carpet.

"I thought you'd escaped out a back window or

something," he said half-jokingly as she came into the room.

She'd been tempted, but she wasn't going to let him know exactly how much he'd unsettled her with his sudden reappearance in her life.

"You said we need to talk?" she answered.

Chloe lowered herself onto the single armchair she possessed and sat stiffly with her hands clasped in her lap, almost as if she'd been called before the principal and was expecting a reprimand. Nervously, she began to chew the inside of her cheek.

Miles moved past her, and the merest waft of the cologne he wore teased her nostrils. She breathed in sharply, then instantly wished she hadn't as her mind was filled with the scent of him and just how close she'd been to him to inhale that particular fragrance. A deep pull of longing dragged through her center and she felt a faint tremor ripple through her body in response. Darn it, how could she let him affect her so easily?

He finally sat down opposite her and leaned forward. She drank in the sight of him, concerned to see that he looked about as rested and happy as she did, which was to say not very much at all.

"Are you okay?" he asked.

She stared at him. She'd betrayed him in the cruelest way and he was asking her if she was okay? Chloe dragged in a deep breath and let it go before answering.

"No, Miles. I'm not okay. How about you?"

The words bounced between them like a tennis ball in a grand slam tournament.

"Me neither. Look, I know I was abrupt with you when you left the estate and I'm sorry. The way I handled that was wrong. I was angry and I didn't listen to you. I owed you that much at least."

"What are you doing here, Miles?" she asked, her voice wreathed with the weariness that pulled at every muscle in her body, including her heart.

"We need to talk… No. Correction. *I* need to talk and I ask that you listen."

Chloe let her body relax against the back of the chair.

"Okay, I'm listening."

He looked at her then, his eyes clashing with hers, and in them she saw a world of hurt meshed with a world of longing. She recognized the look because she saw the same thing in her gaze every morning when she looked in the mirror. Her foolish heart ached for him and what he was going through—for what they both were going through.

"I won't deny that it crushed me to find out that you'd hidden your true motive. I have never in my life felt so betrayed by another person, and believe me, when you grow up with a man like my father, you get used to the feeling. But what you did, it cut me like nothing else I'd ever experienced. I felt as if you'd destroyed us. That you'd torn apart the very fabric of the precious relationship we were building together. I lashed out. And I apologize for that."

She let his words sink in, then parsed through

them. Looking for a glimmer of hope that they could work this thing out between them. But so far, there was not so much as a kernel to cling to. Chloe blinked against the burn of tears that was starting at the back of her eyes and fought not to rub at the sharp pain piercing her chest.

"I'm so sorry I hurt you, Miles. While that might have been my intention— No," she corrected herself. "I have to own this. That *was* my intention—before I met you. But it didn't take me long to realize that you were not the man your father was. My anger and my family's betrayal began and should have ended with Trent Wingate, and I am truly sorry that my mom and I thought we had the right to visit that on you and your brothers and sisters."

She dragged in another breath. "But you hurt me, too. When you confronted me, I told you the truth. I told you everything. I opened up to you and you just slammed a metaphorical door right in my face. You refused to listen to me. You refused to even try to understand what I'd been through and what my life had been like since your father's treatment of my dad, or what motivated me to contemplate doing what I did.

"Choosing that path—revenge—wasn't easy, especially when I discovered exactly who you are on the inside. And knowing who you are and what you're like made it hurt all the more when you turned me away."

Miles's expression twisted, as if he was in pain, and he pressed his lips together as though fighting to hold back words that begged to be said. He closed his eyes briefly and drew in a shuddering breath before opening them again.

"I'm sorry for that, too, Chloe. Believe me, I've never known anyone like you before. The circles my family move in, the people I've mixed with all my life? None of them are like you. Not a single one. I couldn't believe that I could open up and feel about another human being the way I felt about you, right from the start. Do you have any idea what that did to me? You rocked the foundation of my life." Exhaling roughly, he scrubbed a hand across his face. "Yes, of course I know that people meet and fall in love and live happily together forever after. But I always thought that was a pipe dream. Hell, it wasn't even a dream for me. I had my work, I dated. I never expected to fall in love the way I fell for you."

Chloe felt cautious anticipation begin to grow deep inside. Did this mean there was still a chance for them to work through this? To find a way back to each other that had a solid foundation based on truth and love?

"Well, I didn't exactly expect to fall in love with you, either. All my life your family was held up in front of me as a target. As something to bring down. A group of people I didn't know or understand, but people that had destroyed the stability my family had been based on and who forced my father's hand to take his own life. Obviously, now, I understand that no one made that ultimate decision to end my dad's life but him. But that didn't lessen my anger at your family."

"What my father did was despicable, Chloe." Miles shook his head in disbelief. "Even now I can't begin to understand what he was thinking when he did that. *How* he could do that to another human being. But to him, the end always justified the means. When I reached the stage of my life where I understood how he operated was wrong on every level, I distanced myself from him and everything associated with him. I made my own way in the world. Without his support or approval or his money. I am not my father."

"I know, Miles, and I'm sorry I ever thought you were. Of course, when I got to know you, I knew you were not to blame. It made me think twice about what I'd hoped to achieve in hurting you, let alone hurting your entire family. It made me realize that I couldn't go through with it."

They both fell silent for a moment. Each awash in pain and regret. But then Miles shifted and looked at Chloe again. The expression on his face had changed. His eyes held something new. Hope?

"Chloe, answer me this."

"Anything."

"If you were being totally honest with me about your feelings, do you think we can get past this? You brought sunshine in my life in a way I've never experienced before. You blew out the cobwebs and you replaced them all with a breath of fresh air. I've never felt happier with anyone the way I felt when I was with you and, on the flip side, I have never felt as utterly bereft as I have since I ordered you out of my life."

"Of course I was being honest with you, Miles. I fought it. Yes, I'll admit that. But I couldn't help but love you as I started to get to know you. I know you're a proud man—a self-made man—and that you don't need anybody to complete you or your life on any level. But I hope there is room for me in your heart because you fill mine and I wouldn't want it any other way."

He abruptly stood and walked to her chair and pulled her upright.

"Do you mean that? I mean, I'm not doubting you, but this depth of emotion is new to me. I feel like I have to second-guess myself all the time. Today, when I came to find you, I wanted to demand you give me the truth about why you did what you did, but then I realized you'd done that. It was my own stubbornness that refused to listen to what you'd already said."

She lifted her hands and bracketed his face. "Miles, I mean it. I loved you then, I love you now. I will love you forever."

He shuddered then, as if the weight of the world had lifted from his shoulders and he'd finally freed himself from his deepest fear.

"I love you, too, Chloe Fitzgerald. I want to be with you, always. I want to plan a future together with you, a life where we know we can rely on one another and to hell with the rest of the world. We can build our lives together, our own family together—

and all of it on a foundation of truth and happiness. What do you say?"

Tears came to her eyes in earnest now, but she didn't blink them away. These were tears of joy. Of faith in a future she had only ever dreamed of.

"Yes. I say yes!"

He tightened his hold on her and drew her closer, angling his face to hers and capturing her lips in a kiss that imbued all the sweetness of this moment together with all the heat of his love for her and hers for him in return. They might not always have the smoothest road ahead and they still had so much to learn about one another, but Chloe knew in her heart and to the depths of her soul that they'd endure, no matter what.

* * * * *